STRANDED

COIL

Stranded

Coil

Stephanie Hansen

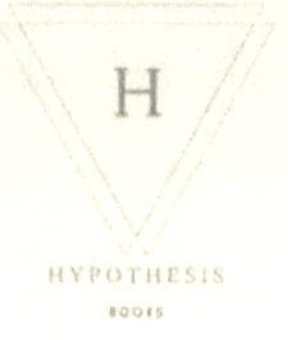

HYPOTHESIS
BOOKS

For my mother, father, and siblings
You have always believed in me even when
I have given you every reason to not.

METAPHASE

When someone you love plans to sacrifice themselves to save innocent people, do you really have a choice? I think so. I think there's always a better answer. Unfortunately, the only answer I can come up with in the time allowed will sacrifice me.

You know those funny old cartoons when the character's floating on a rug or some object in the air, and it's pulled from beneath them? I feel like the character running in place in the air for a couple seconds before the fall.

How do you choose between two people you care about? As time runs out, I have to go ahead and take the leap and hope I've chosen wisely.

DISCOVERY

The bed shakes as Josh jumps from his sleep at my scream. He leaps up to fight an attacker if necessary, but then he sees it's only us in the room. I can hear my heartbeat, it's pounding so hard. He relaxes and puts his arm around me. My room is a mess. The bonus of having a boyfriend from the streets is that he doesn't seem to notice things like that. His forest smell almost causes me to forget my previous thoughts, and I have to hide my smile. How does he make even an undershirt and flannel pajama pants look so attractive? I can see a sheen of sweat on his forehead. I wonder if he'd been having a nightmare in his sleep too.

"Did you have a nightmare?" Josh asks as he gently squeezes me.

My previous thoughts rush back to me. "They're going to go after Jack next if they haven't already done so," I say as I look at him pleadingly. "When did we last see Jack? He wasn't part of the rescue team. I wonder if Lea's with him right now?"

"Why do you think they're after Jack? He was at the haunted house today as we met with security. He even left a little early so he could get Lea a surprise."

I know I should confide in him about everything that has been going on with my father and the warnings, but I'm not ready to yet and, anyway, there's no time. Little Jack, who I couldn't bear to mock hang in the haunted house, is in danger. I think about how he blushes every time he smiles. How he hasn't grown into his extremities, like a puppy with too big paws. Then my mind warps, and I imagine him cut open, even gutted, with blood spilling everywhere. I have to put my head between my legs as I sit to keep the dizzy spell away. I look up and continue talking to Josh because, if there's any way we can save him, we must.

"He has different DNA like mine too. That's why he was hit with the coffee mug that night and a pro-bono medical team magically appeared," I say.

"Are you sure?"

"Dead sure."

##

Tiff and Luke wake easily. I think my scream had already stirred them from their sleep. They make a cute couple in pajamas with matching disheveled hair. We all sit in the kitchen now drinking caffeinated coffee. The smell reminds me of the first day at the haunted house when Josh joined Tiff and me at the coffee shop. Could that really have been just a month ago? It feels like I've known Josh for years now.

"So you think they're after Jack next?" Luke asks as he rubs his eyes.

"I don't have time to explain right now, but yes, they're after him," I confirm.

"Tiff, do you know how to locate him from the restaurant?" Josh asks.

"Um, let me see." She scrolls through the contacts on her phone. "Yeah, here it is. I have his number."

"Call him, Tiff," I beg.

"It's three in the morning. Are you sure?" she asks.

I'm so tired of everyone not believing me. It cuts deep into my pride. Here we've been working together, and this is my best friend, my roommate. They've seen my capabilities, yet now they don't take my word. I guess they think that after being through what I have, my head isn't clear. The stitches in my abdomen still ache. I imagine the men that were going to take my organs and tremble. Josh puts his arm around me and hands me a blanket. I don't feel as tired as I should. I'm alive with fear.

The only thing making me tired is the fact that we're wasting time.

"I'm sure," I state, hoping this ends the questioning.

Tiff hits the green button on her phone. She's like the sister I've never had. She sees that I'm serious now. She puts it on speaker so we can all hear. It rings and rings. After four rings, we're forwarded to his voicemail. Shit. He could be anywhere. He could be safe at home asleep or strapped to a gurney as I'd been. What are we going to do?

"Do you have Lea's number?" I ask frantically.

"She just started working, and I haven't gotten it yet," Tiff answers, giving me a consoling look.

"Should we call the cops?" I plead.

"They should be better able to locate Jack," Tiff says.

"I don't trust them. Why would they help you if I'm involved? They despise the street kids," Josh says. He's looking at the floor as he talks. I put my arm around his shoulders. He has to see that this might be our only hope for some help. I have faith that he can set his distaste aside. They were there when he rescued me, so I'd wished a bridge might have been formed. It looks like it might not be that easy. Past grievances may not be put to rest; ghosts haunting outside of our haunted house.

"I'm with Josh. I've seen cops take payoffs from both Matt and Ed. Who's to say that isn't happening with other parts of the human trafficking ring? I think, if we contact them, we could possibly increase the odds of a bad result for Jack."

Luke's siding with Josh and not with Tiff. This I didn't expect, but what he says makes sense. If he's witnessed it with Matt and Ed, I don't think we have a choice but to find Jack ourselves. I don't know where to begin. The look Josh and Luke give each other reminds me of when kids silently converse behind their parents' backs. They nod their heads as if they understand each other completely without saying a word at all. I wonder what they have up their sleeves.

I wish my father could visit me from the dead as he has recently in my dreams and visions. He had warned me before I was captured. Maybe he could tell me where Jack is. I don't know how to summon him. How does one call the dead, or undead for that matter? I bet Tiff doesn't have that number on her contacts list.

"Tiff, you tailed Matt and Ed to the house and, Luke, you knew about that place before our rescue mission. Do either of you know of other locations?" Josh asks. His forehead creases in concentration. Luke nods at him like he knew this was the direction Josh would take.

"There are two more houses that I know of, but with the arrests that took place, they might have disbanded them," Luke responds.

"Where are they?" I ask.

"Do you have paper and pen?" Luke replies.

Tiff gets up and rifles through the desk in our kitchen. This is where our mail piles up, an abyss of the unknown. It's nice to have a place for that so our table can remain clean and available for meals. The desk is tucked into the wall so as to not make the entire kitchen appear messy. It's so cluttered it's like the black hole of our documents. She's successful in finding paper and pen, though, and returns. Luke draws a map. I recognize some of the downtown streets. He draws a house near Olive and 39th. This is a bit southeast of where we are. The next house is near S. Minnie Street and Lake Avenue. This is southwest of here. Luke's drawing is nowhere close to the intricate artwork Josh could produce, but it's readable, and that's all we need for it to be functional.

"I followed them to the one on Lake Avenue too," Tiff puts in.

"Do we know where Jack's staying? Let's stop by there first, then we can go by the house at Lake Avenue as that's the one we're most familiar with. After that, we can take 39th over to the Olive house," I say.

I'm ready to be doing something. Every second that passes worries me. I find myself massaging my hands to release tension.

"We should get some help. Can we stop by Ethan's first?" Josh asks. There's a hint of resignation in his words, but Luke's nodding his head in approval. This must have been what they had up their sleeves. They want more people on this mission. I can't really complain, but what time could it cost us and how much does Jack have left if he's taken?

"That's out of the way," I reply, exasperated.

"We can go to Jack's place first and then to the house on Olive," Josh says.

"But Luke and Tiff both have witnessed the Lake Avenue house. I think we run the risk of losing Jack if we don't go to the Lake Avenue house first. If we go to the Olive house, they'll tip off the Lake Avenue house and relocate Jack to an unknown place," I say.

"Or they *could* be at the Olive house to keep a low profile after the arrests of their colleagues," Tiff says. "If they've been watching us as closely as I fear, I may have tipped them off when I followed them to the Lake Avenue house. I'm sorry."

I hate when Tiff apologizes to me. It's not like she's part of this human trafficking ring. What does she have to be sorry for? She followed her intuition and tailed them to see what was going on. She's been more aware than I apparently have been.

She's right. It's a huge possibility. We really have no clue where they are. We have to split up.

"Okay. Let's recruit more people and split up. We can simultaneously approach both houses," I suggest.

Luke and Josh nod their heads again as if this was expected. Maybe Josh even led me down this trail on purpose. Then Luke looks at me.

"Um, Austria, are you up for this? You just got out of the hospital. They were already after you. Won't we run the risk of them recapturing you?" Luke states.

I see the muscles around Josh's jaw flex. His hands clench into fists too. I grab one of his hands and massage it open, out of the fist, hoping to release the tension as I had in my own.

"I'll be okay. I'll stay out of their reach. Now, can we go already?"

DEBATE

We pile into Luke's Escape. It oddly feels like we're a couple of husbands and wives setting out on a Sunday drive. If only we were enjoying something that relaxing. His car even has a new car smell. Instead, we're driving to Jack's apartment, hoping to find him asleep and not kidnapped by people who want his organs. Just the thought of it makes my breath catch. Jack lives in an apartment within a tall building across 31st from Penn Valley Community College. The gray cement feels like a prison. It towers over us and curves around us. It gets cold as thunderclouds blot out the sun. We buzz his number. Luckily, Tiff had the apartment number saved in her phone too, in hopes that he'll answer, and all of the worrying tonight will be for nothing.

"Hello." It's a girl's voice.

"Lea," I say.

"Yeah? What are you doing out and about? Shouldn't you be resting?" she asks.

"Can you let us up? It's me, Josh, Tiff, and Luke."

There's a click, then we open the building door, and head up to Jack's place. The stairs are laminate with black rubber footholds. The stairway's depressing and dark. It smells dusty. The metal railings are cold to the touch. I'm glad we only have to climb three stories. My abdomen aches with each step, but if I say anything, they'll put me back in the last place I want to be, bed. I'm glad I'm at the rear of the group so I can wobble up the stairs attempting to scale them without using abdominal muscles. I feel like a pregnant woman. Lea lets us in when we're at the door to Jack's apartment.

"What's up? Have you seen Jack? I've been looking all over for him. He isn't at any of our secret hangouts." She blushes with the last statement. She's adorable. Jack and her both are. She looks flustered. Her hands are shaking. Her hair is in disarray.

"No, that's actually why we came here," Tiff says.

"Shoot. But your group doesn't always hang with him. Why would you come all the way here?" There's a wall of silence. We all glance at each other awkwardly. She looks at us one by one. She gasps for breath. Luke rushes over to her and has her sit down.

"What is it? What aren't you telling me?" Lea says shakily.

Everyone looks uneasy. Lea's eyes get so wide, I'm afraid they might pop out of her head.

"Lea, do you remember Jack being hit over the head with the coffee mug and the pro-bono medical team?" I ask.

"Uh, yeah. What does that have to do with anything?"

"Jack has different DNA." I pause. I'm completely breaking our promise to my mother. I wish I didn't have to tell so many people about my DNA being different, but I don't see how I can explain this and its urgency to Lea without doing so. "I know because I do too. The same people who had me are after Jack."

"Oh. Wait, so do they have him now? This is out of control. We have to find him." Lea's putting on a jacket and her shoes. Her jacket is leather, and her shoes of choice are sturdy boots. These outside appearances contrast with her trembling hands. Now I feel like Luke. He'd thought it might be best for me to stay back and not join in the search. That had really upset me, but here I am thinking the same thing of

Lea. She really isn't in the best emotional state for a rescue mission.

I walk over to her and put my hands on her shoulders so she has to look me straight in the eyes. She appears as impatient as I had felt earlier tonight. I take a deep breath. "Lea, you need to be able to keep your head if you go with us. Can you do that?"

She follows my lead and takes a deep breath and exhales. Her eyes focus on mine. "I'm fine," she says. I can see why Lea was able to work at the haunted house. The look she gives me tells me that if I try to stop her, I may lose a limb. Not as sweet and innocent as my first impression of her had implied.

We're back in Luke's Escape headed to Ethan's place. His mom is still out of town. I wonder what he, Patrice, and probably Ceresa are doing right now. I rest my head against the window next to me and look up at the stars. I find the Big Dipper and the North Star. The North Star falls behind us as we head south, like the hand of a clock. It's four in the morning. If we take much longer, we're not going to be able to sneak up on the houses in the dark.

When we pull up to Ethan's house, I see more lights on than I'd been expecting. He must have people over. This could throw a wrench in our plans. The three peaks of the roof appear to be reaching toward the sky more than the last time we were here. We all exit the Escape and head to the door. It opens before any of us knock.

Ethan greets us, "Did you hear what happened? Is that why you're here?"

"No, man. What happened?" Josh asks as we all enter.

Then I see Camille on the couch in the Game/Dining Room. She has a small towel up to her face. The towel is drenched in blood. Emmitt's by her side massaging her shoulders and neck. Brittany and Landon are on the floor playing a video game. Patrice and Ceresa walk out of the kitchen toward us. Patrice has another towel, and Ceresa has a baggie of ice.

"Hola, see the bloody nose our coworkers dragged in here," Patrice says.

"What are all of you doing here? We've had enough action tonight," Ceresa complains as she removes the bloody towel from Camille's face to inspect her nose. Luke walks over to examine her. Without his medical school experience, I may not have survived my kidnapping. I have him to thank for my very professional sutures.

"Jack's missing. We're sure he's been taken by the same group that took me. There are two possible locations that we need to seek out." I eye them and hope my words are sinking in. I don't have time to explain this more than once. What if they think I'm hiding something? Would they really think I would do that right after they saved me? Just as in the beginning, I'm questioning my read on people, but I am hiding something from them. I've been seeing shadows and my dead/undead dad.

"Why would they take Jack? Are we all doomed to this fate? Why are they targeting us?" Patrice asks viciously. Her shoulders have tensed.

"They're not after all of us. Only the ones with different DNA," I say. And here we go, more explaining.

"What are you talking about?" Ceresa asks. She has grabbed Patrice's hand.

I know we promised my mother that we would keep the secret, but I've already told so many. I might as well tell my entire haunted house family. I feel goosebumps rise on my forearms.

"Jack and I have different DNA. We have Altered Helixes. It isn't really that big of a deal. We heal faster, so that's why we've been targeted. I guess the investors in the stolen organs want ones that heal quickly."

"Whoa. Are you like the Wolverine or something? I had wondered how you were able to be here so quickly after being cut open," Ethan chimes in. He punches Josh in the arm with brotherly love.

"Like I said, it's really not that big of a deal. Plus it makes me dizzy sometimes. Remember when I fainted," I say.

"Wait a minute," Camille says. "Did you just say dizzy? I carry mints in my purse all the time because I have fainting spells. The reason why I have a bloody nose is because I was attacked earlier tonight. We'd all been walking home to our place, and I fell behind. This stupid man grabbed me from behind. He tried to cover my mouth and nose with a cloth, but I got a good elbow in his ribs first. I've studied ka- rate and other self-defense techniques, but he was still able to hit me in the nose. As soon as I had him down, Emmitt, Brittany and Landon were with me, and we ran." She seems to be awestruck.

Josh and I exchange a glance when she mentions that a man tried to cover her mouth and nose with a cloth. That's how I had been taken, and he had witnessed it. Too bad I didn't have reflexes like Camille. Maybe we wouldn't even be in this mess if I would've been able to fight back. I feel a pang of guilt in my stomach. We have to get Jack.

"So I have different DNA like you?" she asks.

"I think these occurrences lean toward that fact," I say as I try to calm myself down.

"Did you recognize anything about your attacker?" I continue.

Camille twisting a strand of hair in her fingers as she concentrates. "Come to think of it, I think I saw the man at the blood donation center."

I'm in shock now. Camille must have an Altered Helix too. I cannot believe three of us have different DNA. I'd thought I was a freak, but it seems to be more prevalent than I had realized.

"All right, you three are like blood siblings. Great. Can we please go get Jack? I'm so afraid for him," Lea pleads, pacing back and forth.

"You're right, Lea. We can discuss our DNA later. It just startled me for a second. Let's get Jack," Camille responds reassuringly.

"Okay, Luke, you've been inside these places. Can you give me the general layout of the floor plan?" Josh asks. As usual, he's keeping us on target. He knows just how to make a comment that will get the ball rolling in the direction we need. His forehead creases yet again.

Luke draws out the floor plans to complement the previous drawings of locations. Ceresa makes sure he marks where the windows are. We may need to visit Gunner and get more ether and gas masks so we can knock out the bad guys again and save Jack the way they saved me. Lea wants to see doorways and other points of entry and exit. I try to split us into two equal groups since going to the cops is out of the question. Our biggest guys are Ethan and Emmitt. They both have experience fighting, so one will be in each group. Luke and Landon are next. I put Luke with Ethan and Landon with Emmitt as they already know each other. I see the flaw here. Who's going to treat Jack if he's cut and Luke isn't in their group?

"Does anyone besides Luke have medical experience?" I ask everyone.

"I went to nursing school," Brittany says.

I put Tiff and Brittany with Emmitt and Landon. That leaves Camille, Lea, Josh, and I. Tiff can't be in Luke's group as they are the two who know the locations. When I say this out loud, I see the pain in Luke's and Tiff's eyes as they look at each other. To even things out, I put Lea and myself with Ethan. Josh speaks up and states that he should be with me and Lea. I can tell he's being protective, and I want to protest, but Camille will feel more comfortable with her group. I think Ceresa will be good with that group too as she has medical experience on the streets. I see the look of relief on Ethan's and Patrice's faces as they see they'll be grouped together.

I try to tell them as much about my experience as I can so they're prepared, but my memory is fuzzy. I remember the chloroform, but Camille's own story about chloroform is newer than mine. Plus, we unfortunately are more than likely past that point. I tell the group that I think the gurney will be in a place like a basement away from windows and where possible screams may not be heard easily outside of the house. Luke fills Brittany in on the two shots that he had used on me. They'd been available for him when he rescued me. Do we hope the same will hold true for Jack, or do we try to get them from Gunner with the ether? If he doesn't have these things right on him, I'm afraid we don't have time to collect them elsewhere.

We assign someone to man a phone for each group. There'll be a call between the groups, so we unleash the ether on each house at the same time. There will also be a phone call when Jack's found. The person manning the phone for the group that doesn't find Jack will call Bill and ask him to notify the authorities because, by that point, even if they've been paid off, it will be too late for them to be a danger to Jack. We all study the layout drawings Luke put together. I feel like I am part of a S.W.A.T. team strategizing to secure a hostage situation. It's kind of exciting, but a blanket of anguish smothers us. We're experienced in haunting, not in rescue missions. I wish we could call an adult, like Bill, but I know if we do, they won't pay heed to our misgivings about the police. They would call them at the first chance.

"Okay, I think we've planned this out the best we can. Let's go get Jack," Lea almost yells.

CAPTURE

We have to backtrack to get to Gunner at the market, but in order to keep us all safe and give Jack the best chance of recovery, it's a must. It is like our own version of the SWAT team's armored tank. The market's quite busy, even at this hour, and I'm afraid of all of the people that surround us. We can't chance anyone overhearing our game plan. What if they're somehow connected to the human trafficking ring? My fear subsides when I see Gunner. He has a crew cut and wears army fatigues that are tattered from years of use. I don't know why I had envisioned him with messy long hair and looking deranged. His eyes are bright and, the second his gaze meets Josh's, he ushers us over to a more secluded spot. Two for two, Gunner has his wits about him again. Thank goodness. We had not made a backup plan if we couldn't get the ether from him. I hope our plans don't have any more holes than that.

We separate from there. I find it difficult to watch Tiff go in the group that's not my own. My group is in Luke's Escape. Ethan and Luke are in the front while Lea, Patrice, Josh, and I are crammed in the back. Lucky for Lea and Patrice, I'm in Josh's lap shrunk down so we aren't pulled over. Emmitt has a full-size van for the other team. No one has to sit on anyone's lap in that vehicle. Not that I honestly mind sitting on Josh's lap. It's reassuring to be so close to him before we encounter danger. My own version of the SWAT helmet and bulletproof vest. What are we thinking, attempting this on our own? It worked before and I hope, despite all odds, it works again. The ride seems to make everyone thoughtful, for it is silent. Lea keeps biting her fingernails. Ethan is pounding a tune on the dashboard like he's playing the drums. Patrice is looking at him with an appraising smile. Josh and I hold hands, as if praying for the success of our next actions.

We make it to the Olive house; the other team went to the Lake Avenue house because that's the one Tiff is familiar with. We pile out of the car and stretch our legs. We are a little ways down the street so as to not be detected. We walk to the house in an even larger silence than the one we had travelled in. A shadow flies across the street. My breath catches. I'd only been seeing shadows in the haunted house. No one else seems to have noticed it. I'm not sure if these shadows are just straight up following me or if they appear when danger's near, but it sends a shiver through me either way. I'm grateful for Josh's hand in mine. I squeeze, and he holds tighter.

When we're next door, we crouch behind a bush away from the streetlight.

"The windows are open again. What is it with this group?" Luke asks as he peers around to view the house.

Lea, Patrice, and I take turns running hoses to the windows. We're the smallest and can move the easiest undetected. The house sits on top of a small grassy hill. It has brick with white side panels from the top of the first floor to the roof. The windows are within reach. They have metal frames and must be at least twenty years old. I'm grateful they're open. I know these old windows creak when opened, and I don't think we could've opened them without being noticed. We should acquire some glass cutters. Once the hoses are in place, Patrice calls Ceresa while the rest of us put gas masks on.

"We're ready," Patrice whispers.

She gives a thumbs up, and Josh turns the switch that forces the ether into the house.

"Talk to you soon." Patrice hangs up the phone and puts on her own gas mask.

When Josh had made his testimony of how they saved me, I had not been able to understand fully what he meant by hearing bodies hit the floor. Now I do. How intense is that? I know some of these guys are large, but to be able to hear their bodies hit the floor out here is astonishing. I guess dead weight can do that. We all jog to the closest window of the house. Ethan pries it all the way open. Lucky for us, this window isn't behind bars as many in this neighborhood are. Maybe we should also acquire some metal cutters. That's another thing we had not planned for. I hope the Lake Avenue house doesn't have bars on all the windows.

Once we're inside, and the perimeter has been checked, Ethan gives us a thumbs up.

"The way to the basement is over here," Luke says.

We all head that way as quietly as we can. Josh opens the door and peeks his head in to be sure the coast is clear. He turns back to us and nods. Then we descend the stairs. I can hear my heart beating in my ears when I spot the gurney. That brings back memories I would be glad to forget. Everyone seems to sense my uneasiness, and they spot the gurney too. They walk to it. It's empty. I still haven't managed to move my feet. It's as if they have dried in cement.

Another shadow flies by me, right in front of my face. If I were faster, I would've reached out to touch it. It flies up to the ceiling and then through the crack under a door. I remember the room they kept me in before hauling me to the gurney when I attempted to escape. I'd spent a long time conscious and unconscious in that room. That's where Jack is. It has to be. I have to get to him. I remember how alone I felt in that room. My feet are free now, having somehow rid themselves of the cemented feeling. I run to the door. As I open it, I hear Josh say "No." I take a step in ,and someone grabs my arm. They pull me into the room, shut the door and lock it. It's so dark I can't see a thing. Then I feel the all-too-familiar prick of a needle penetrating my arm. My body goes limp, but I'm awake. I still cannot see anything.

My assailant throws me over their right shoulder. On the back of the assailant's head are straps from a breathing mask. My eyes have adjusted to the dark. It seems they did somewhat prepare for a possible rescue mission. I'm surprised they still left the windows open. Had it all been a trick to lure us in? Then I feel a hand hit mine. I look to my left with my eyes only as my head won't move and see Jack in the same position as myself but on the opposite shoulder. Here I am another victim when I was supposed to be helping Jack. At least the paralyzing sensation numbs the pain I would feel with my attacker's shoulder gouging into my abdomen. I'm so sorry, Jack. Maybe they'd only wanted to lure those with different DNA. They had to know I'd be the one to recognize the room first. I feel something clutch my heart. It's the grief of my errors. Here my friends had come to save Jack, and I just led myself straight into the lion's den. Maybe they'd been right after all about my ability to help in their mission.

No, I will not let this happen. Then my assailant climbs a few steps and pushes something with their head. Two doors swing open, and we're crawling out of the earth next to the house. This is not a good sign. They could take Jack and me to an unidentified place and have twice the organs. What can I do? Father, help.

I see a flash as Ethan tackles the assailant. He's faster than I thought. Jack and I tumble to the ground, still unable to move. The assailant rises and grabs something out of his jacket while heading in Ethan's direction, but Patrice hits the attacker in the back of the head with a pipe. I can see Ethan smile at Patrice. He runs up, and she jumps into his arms. The others come shortly after that and help carry Jack and me to the car. We pile in, and Luke starts the engine and peels out.

Luke's driving, and Patrice is in the front passenger seat. Lea's in the middle of the back. Ethan is to her left with Jack in his lap. Ethan sees Lea's need and lays Jack's head in her lap so she can brush his hair with her fingers. I'm in Josh's lap. He holds me like a child. I see the terror in his eyes when my head flops from one side to the other. I have no control. I wish I could make it stop so he could be at ease. He takes his hand and holds my head on his shoulder. We're speeding down the street. Patrice calls Ceresa so her group will know we have Jack and can call Bill. She never speaks. She hangs up the phone.

"No answer?" Luke asks, concerned.

I bet they're still looking for Jack, but it's odd that they aren't answering. I hope they haven't run into issues like us. Oh shoot, did they get Camille? I recognize how flawed our plans had been, but we do have Jack.

"We have to go to the hospital," Luke says. "St. Luke's on Broadway is closest. There'll be authorities there. I know you Streets don't like the cops, but the hospital's such a public place, they'll have to help us; bribes, Streets, or not. I haven't been able to ascertain if Jack's injured. Both Jack and Austria need shots to take the paralysis out of them."

Just then, the phone rings. Ceresa is so loud that even I can hear her, and she's not on speakerphone.

"We didn't see Jack. They woke up, Patrice. Some wore gas masks. It was like they knew we were coming. Tiff got cut. We had to get out of there. They're tailing us. What do we do?"

"Go to St. Luke's on Broadway. That's where we're headed too. We have Jack," Patrice says, but she doesn't hang up. I think Ceresa and her need to hear each other to know they're safe. Patrice stares at the phone.

"We're being tailed too," Luke says as he floors it.

We screech into the hospital emergency parking lot at the same time as the others. Our tails speed off into the night. Looks like the crowded hospital scene was a good choice on Luke's part. I see both groups exit their vehicles as my head rests on Josh's shoulder looking out. Everyone's hugging each other. Tiff almost knocks Luke down when she runs and jumps into his arms. He smells her hair and smiles. Guess the cut wasn't too bad, but I still watch to be sure she isn't vitally injured. Luke says something to her I cannot hear, and she shows him a gaping hole in her shirt. He lifts it, and I can tell she's going to need stitches. Josh is holding me and walking to the entrance.

"Ethan, thank you for carrying Jack," Lea says.

Hospital staff surrounds us now, putting Jack and me on gurneys and attending to Tiff. I know this is a safe gurney, but the feeling still makes me sick to my stomach. We're rolled into the hospital. I think I hear a nurse say Tiff just needs ten stitches and with Luke's look of agreement, I'm relieved. At least Tiff wasn't harmed too badly, but I detest putting the ones so close to me in such a situation. I have to find an end to this so they can live the lives they're meant to live. I hear Luke telling them what he believes we were injected with and what he used last time to wake me. I can feel them work on me, and I can see Josh's look of concern, but I feel disconnected. I can't be going into shock again. It wasn't like last time. It wasn't quite as scary because I knew I wasn't alone this time. I can't help myself. I have to close my eyes and try to get a grip.

"You're safe. This has to change. You're putting too much at risk." My father's back. I don't know if I fell asleep and am dreaming or if it is like the out-of-body experience when I fainted. I do not see my body from above so I must be in shock and dreaming, or whatever you call this.

"Father, I don't understand what's going on. Why, now, are they after us all? Why are you able to talk to me so much lately?"

"I didn't have time to explain earlier, but I do now. At least I can explain part of it. They are after you because you have different DNA. The results of that don't fully set in until you're between the ages of seventeen and twenty-two. These differences caused by your DNA don't manifest themselves until you have the ability to recognize future consequences, which is after the frontal lobe fully develops in the human brain. I was unable to communicate with you until you reached this point. Plus, we're better able to converse when you are at dangerous moments because of the way adrenaline kicks the special abilities you have pushing your DNA to another level."

"Okay. So why did you disappear? What are you?"

"Oh, you're waking up now. I love you. Talk to you later."

"I love you too, Father."

That was weird. He just said "talk to you later" like he knows we'll be conversing soon. He also said that it's easier to speak to me in times of danger. Does that mean I'll be in danger again soon? When will it end?

My closed eyelids look bright red from the hospital lights. I hear the sound of a monitor beeping next to me. I feel Josh's hand on mine. I slowly open my eyes. He's asleep in a chair next to my bed with his head resting on the bed. I take my hand from under his and begin patting his head. He wakes up disoriented.

"You're okay. I knew you shouldn't go with us. What would I have done if that man had gotten away with you and Jack?"

"What would you have done if they'd come after me while I was alone, and you guys were off to rescue Jack?" I ask while raising my other hand up to the sky with a bend at my elbow and shrug.

He smiles. I put my hand on his cheek and smile back at him. "I'm fine, Josh. How's Jack?"

"He's in a state of shock. What is with you DNA people and shock?"

"I don't know. I'm trying to find out." I've gone too far. The only way I've been trying to find out is through my father and I haven't told anyone about that.

"Oh yeah, how are you doing that?"

I'm silent. I don't know how to back-track and cover my misstep.

"Austria?"

"It's a long story."

"Doesn't look like we're going any-where soon."

I tell him about how my father has been contacting me lately. Much of his contact has been warnings. I tell him about how I'm unsure if my father is really dead, but that I only see him when I'm not in completely conscious states. My father's appeared in dreams, out-of-body experiences, and as a hazy figure in a mirror reflection. I worry that Josh will look at me like I'm crazy, but he never does. I tell him that I fear there's more to come given my father's confidence in seeing me again. Then I have to explain that the adrenaline rush caused by fear allows us to communicate easier. While he has the look of understanding and reassurance I'd been hoping for, I catch another look pulling him from within. He's jealous. He lost his parents and never had a relationship with them. Not only do I have a living and supportive mother, but my father's trying to help me from the dead or whatever he is.

"At least they're not after you for your organs," I say as I brush his cheek with my fingers.

He puts his hand on mine and holds it against his cheek. He looks me in the eyes. My monitor beeps faster. He looks at it and then at me. I do believe my heart rate is about to the maximum it's allowed before the nurses outside my room are notified. He smiles, but then his face turns serious.

"If you think for a second, I wouldn't rather them be after my organs than your organs, you don't understand how much I care for you."

"Josh, don't say that."

"What would society lose if my organs were stolen? It's not like I'm an upstanding citizen with collegiate aspirations. Hell, society would probably benefit more from my donated organs than from me living."

"Stop. Don't say things like that. If anything were to happen to you, it would be the end of me. I would be crushed. I wouldn't be able to give anything. You give more to this world than you give yourself credit for. I've seen the way you support people and inspire them to have the courage to fight for their dream."

"Oh, Austria, you're like the family I never had. I don't know what I'd do without your belief in me," he whispers as if telling a secret.

"What about Ceresa, Ethan, and Patrice? They're like family, and they believe in you."

"It's not the same."

"Okay, let's just agree to keep each other safe the best we can."

"I will try to help you figure out what's going on with your father. You can talk to me about anything." He leans over the hospital bed and hugs me.

STATUS QUO

Once Jack and I fully recover, we return to the haunted house. The organ at the entrance isn't as terrorizing as it once was. Though the pipes still tower above me, they don't seem as foreboding. Instead, they seem like a wall of comfort, like my mother really should be sitting there playing *Beautiful Torment*. Even the dark rooms and props of evil seem to have lost their eerie luster. Everyone looks as if we're returning home. Everyone applauds as we walk in. Jack runs and picks up Lea. This different DNA really does give us better healing capabilities.

The others have been able to somewhat cover our spots while we've been gone. Bill now wants us to run through a rehearsal with everyone in their original places. There's also a new element to the house that Jack and I aren't used to. We now have guards at appointed positions within the house. We need to rehearse getting from one place to another while checking in with the guards. In order to remain concealed, they get to wear costumes too. It's comical to see Ceresa putting makeup on these tough guys. The smallest one has to be at least two hundred and fifteen pounds and six feet tall. It feels as though we've re-cruited a football team to join the haunted house staff.

Everything comes back slowly. I re-member my parts and placements but find it difficult to act. I've been so petrified lately, I find it hard to ignore my inner emo-tions. Jack seems to pick up everything faster. His acting ability helps. Ceresa coaches me if I falter. After mock-hanging Jack, I remember that we lost Matt and Ed. We had skipped over the part of Ceresa taking cyanide. I don't know if Matt and Ed are in jail or out. The thought of them being out freezes me. Jack seems to notice and puts his hand on my shoulder.

"Everything okay?" he asks me just like a brother would.

I have to clear my throat to talk. "Yeah. Matt used to ride a chariot at this point. Do you know where Matt and Ed are?"

Ceresa answers for him. "Don't worry. Tiff made sure to file restraining orders against them for this location, your place, and Ethan's. I found a couple street kids to fill their spots. We have guards. Everything will be okay."

I take a deep breath. "So, they are out. That's intense. I wonder what their parents had to pay for that. Thank you guys for putting up protections and finding replacements."

Ceresa did find a stocky guy to replace Matt. He stops by us before mounting the chariot.

"Hi, um, I'm Brian." He offers his hand awkwardly for me to shake. I like him already. His personality is about the complete opposite of cocky Matt's.

I shake his hand. His shake is firm but not overbearing. I smile at him. "It's nice to meet you, Brian. Thank you for filling in last minute."

"Not a problem. Ceresa has helped me out more than a couple times. Plus, it'll be nice to fill my pockets before winter."

I'd almost forgotten the street kids' troubles while concentrating on my own. Here they've gone out of their way to help me and what have I done for them? I don't care what my past perceptions of the street kids had been. I've found them to be some of the most selfless people I've ever known. Once again, I find myself grateful for this opportunity. Then Brian's on the chariot, and we all prepare to run. Jack flips the switch to the water for the "splitting of the sea" scene. The lit water rushes through the glass panes. It makes me think of being cleansed. I feel like, with these people, my haunted house people, I could be cleansed of the fear and pain that's filled the past few days.

I smile as Jack runs screaming through the doorway and into the hall. I join with everyone running. My heart races but not in fear. I look forward to seeing the rest of the rooms, but Bill has an announcement. He tells our group to head to the inventory room. We're having a meeting.

As I walk into the room, Josh catches up to me and grabs my hand. I take my arm and hook it into his so we're closer. He smiles at me as he brushes a bit of dust from my shoulder. The sight of vanity after vanity is not as impressive as before, but it now is filled with memories. Memories bonding with the street girls in our pursuit to put Matt and Ed in place. Memories of seeing my father. The haunted house feels like returning home after a vacation. It's familiar and warm. We sit on a box in the center. Others sit on the chairs and boxes or stand. Bill's in the center. I see he now has a Carhartt coat over his flannel. It enriches his rough exterior that I know covers his true and kind interior.

"You've done an excellent job today. To see you jump back from such dire circumstances gives an old man hope. Thank you for being you. I don't want to push those who have been through so much too soon, so we're breaking for lunch. I don't have food so you're free to do as you choose. You have two hours today."

We all look at each other amazed. Bill's never given us two hours for lunch. Our group has grown, and I'm not sure we'll find a place to fit us all. Ethan, Patrice, Ceresa, Josh, myself, Tiff, Jack, Lea, Camille, Emmitt, Brittany, and Landon head out the door trying to come up with a solution. A party of twelve is going to find it difficult to be seated at a table last minute. Oh, and we have a guard assigned to us for lunch too. That makes thirteen. We decide to go to Zaina and get food to go to eat at Tiff's and my place.

Zaina is packed as usual, but their service is also quick. People are bustling through. Many come from the street. Some come from the walking bridge over Walnut. On one wall, there's a mural of a Mediterranean city on luscious green hills with mountains in the background. I'd been too busy to notice that before. We're waiting for our food when Camille and Brittany break from the group to use the restroom. Our guard asks them to be quick. Conversation resumes about parties that had been scared in the previous nights.

"This kid jumped back three feet when I scared him. I thought he was going to take out half of his friends," Landon says through a laughing fit.

"That was nothing. I swear the one with the pink Mohawk peed his pants," Emmitt adds with wide eyes of disbelief.

I can't help but laugh with them. It's fun to scare when it's not in harmful ways. I notice it has been awhile and look toward the bathroom to see if Camille and Brittany are headed back. What I see takes the oxygen right from me. Brittany is by herself walking back to our group. She has a confused look on her face.

"What kind of trick is this, Camille?" Brittany asks, looking between us like she's trying to find Camille. "You've got to be kidding me!"

"What are you talking about? Isn't Camille with you?" I ask her.

"Great, you're going to play along with Camille's trick. Like we haven't had enough to fret about recently. That is SO funny."

"No, really, she's not out here. Are you sure she's not still in the restroom?"

"Crap. I looked everywhere and didn't see her."

The guard now starts his way to the restroom. He knocks and, when no one replies, enters the restroom. I follow him. He looks in one stall while I look in the other. We turn circles to see if there's another place someone could be. There aren't any windows. There isn't a closet. I look up, but the ceiling doesn't have a possible exit either. It's a complete ceiling, not a false one made of rectangles that can be moved to access a crawlspace.

"This doesn't make sense. There's no way she could have left," he says after checking the stall I'd checked.

As we return to the group, I hear everyone debating.

"This isn't a funny trick if that's what you two are doing, Brittany," Emmitt says.

"This isn't a trick. I don't know where she is. I swear," Brittany answers as Landon puts his arms around her.

"I think she's done it again," Jack says.

"Done what?" Lea asks.

"She told me that she thought there was something else the ones with special DNA could do. We can heal fast, we faint, and we can see and become shadows," Jack answers.

"What?" I ask. "What do you mean by see and become shadows?"

"I know you've seen the shadows too. Like when you were startled and told me you had forgotten something back in the inventory room. I saw it too."

"I kind of figured that out, Jack. That's one of the reasons I knew they were after you too. What I don't get is the part about 'becoming' shadows."

"When Camille visited me at the hospital, she mentioned out-of-body experiences and a close to death encounter. She said she was able to be invisible to others apart from people like us being able to see her shadow. She could converse with people that weren't really there. She said it felt different. It was almost like she was a spirit."

I remember the out-of-body experience I had when I fainted at the haunted house and talked with my "dead" father. This all has something to do with my DNA. Guess that makes sense to me. Then I remember when I'd almost died on the gurney and went into shock, or at least that's what it seemed to be. I remember feeling like a different being and sympathizing things such as the wind that has no control over where it blows.

This really is the time to choose. I've already shared so much with everyone here. Now I'm not the only person going through it. They can't treat me like a freak the way I fear they will. Even though they are my friends, people can only understand so much outside the norm. It's time to confide in them all. I'm glad Josh knows about my father talking to me. I wish I'd told him everything.

"Um, yeah, but I didn't realize I was becoming a shadow during those times," I say.

"So you've had the experience. I haven't. What's it like?" Jack asks.

"Camille was right when she said it's like becoming a spirit. I felt things I've never felt before. I've been able to communicate with my father, who *died* when I was fourteen."

"Wow. That sounds exciting. Can I try?" Jack asks.

"What I don't understand is that during my experiences my body has been where people could see it. When I fainted, you guys could see me, but I was looking above and over my body and the group. When I was in shock, people still saw me in the hospital. We can't find Camille anywhere."

"So can Camille get back now that her body is gone too?" a very worried Emmitt asks.

"I…don't know," I state flatly. I wish there were more I could offer, but I truly do not know.

DISAPPEAR

"What do we do? Do we leave without her? Our two hours is almost up," Jack says.

We all had pretty much lost our appetites with Camille's disappearance. We only make an attempt to eat outside of Zaina, instead of going to my place, to keep our strength so we can search for her.

"You all head back. I'll wait here to see if she returns. If she doesn't after an hour, I'm going to check all of our usual places. What if when she comes back she doesn't get to choose where?" Emmitt asks. He looks as lost as Camille is.

"I'll stay with you for protection. The rest of you stay in your group until you're back to the haunted house with the other guards," the guard says.

"The shadows seem to be able to place themselves near others like them or near danger. I think she'll either return here, at your regular places, or at the haunted house, Emmitt," I say, trying to reassure him.

The rest of us head back to the haunted house. We're unsure what to tell Bill, but I feel since the rest of the haunted house family knows, Bill should too. Bill's at a loss when we try to explain what happened.

"Well, I guess we'll finish the rehearsals with Ceresa and Patrice taking Camille's roles where they can. Are you sure she wasn't taken, and we shouldn't be going after her?" Bill asks.

"There was no way she could have exited without us seeing her," I say.

"Wasn't it busy and there were thirteen of you," he answers.

"I don't see that as possible. The way Zaina is laid is somewhat like a galley. There's just no way she could've left. Plus

Brittany didn't hear her exit the restroom that we all saw them go in." Josh backs up my claim.

"All right, let's finish up rehearsals. I'm worn out already," Bill says.

We finish the day's work without the enthusiasm we had begun with. The roles seem tedious when we all are tormented by where Camille could be. Patrice and Ceresa do a pretty good job of covering for her, but there's no way they can do this and make it to their roles and check-ins in time when we're live. Camille has to return by tomorrow, or we're doomed.

We finish and Bill calls a wrap. We head home with our heads held low.

"I'm calling Emmitt to see if he's found anything," Brittany says.

We all freeze and wait in silence for the answer.

"Have you come across anything? No, she didn't show up here. Okay. See you at the apartment." Brittany hangs up her phone.

Landon gives her a hug. We all head home.

"Can I call you in the morning to see if she's appeared?" Tiff asks Brittany.

"Sure. I just don't understand. What can we do?" Brittany says.

"Just keep yourselves safe. I'm going to see if I can contact her through the night," I say.

"Thank you," Brittany exclaims. The look of despair that I see on her face makes me revert to primitive behavior. I clutch my arms around myself as if I can shield away the evil haunting us. My adrenaline picks up a little, and I want to investigate every sound and sight.

At home Tiff, Luke, Josh, and I get ready for bed. No news turned up during dinner or the hour after. Josh walks with me to my room. We sit up and talk for a while.

I sit on my bed with my knees cradled to my chest. He rubs my back.

"I just get a weird sense that my father understands what's going on. Maybe this is the explanation for how he could disappear and not die, but he's never returned in the flesh that I know of. What if Camille can't return either?" I say while my eyes dart around beyond my control.

"We'll figure something out. We won't be any help to them if we don't get the rest we need, though. Do you need some chamomile tea to help you sleep?" Josh asks. He's so caring. How many guys would think to ask a girl if she needs tea to relax?

"That would be great, Josh. Thanks," I say as I lie down.

I don't know if he brings back the tea. I'm asleep before he has the chance. All of the commotion of the day petered me out. My father's talking to me before I even realize I'm asleep.

"Your friend is with us. We're the shadows you see. We're trying to warn you of precarious situations," my father says.

"Camille's with you? Is she okay? Can she come back?"

"Yes, and yes she's okay. She can come back, but it's a little difficult right now. She didn't come here alone. See the people after you in your world have members like us that can travel between worlds too. One of them came after Camille in the bathroom, and that's why she disappeared. We have her safe from the one who went after her, but it's rather trying to teach her how to travel back, since she travelled here against her free will."

"What world, where are you? How long do you think it will take for her to learn?"

"Telling you about my world is a little difficult. Camille's working real hard. I think she should be back by tomorrow."

"Oh, that's good. So how many of our enemies have the ability to travel too?"

"Quite a few, but don't worry. We have it under control."

"Are they after you guys there, too? Can you come back to your body and be with us again, Father?"

"Please don't concern yourself, Austria. Get some rest."

"Wait, I don't understand, and I want to know."

"I'm sorry. We're running out of time. I only get a small window with you each visit."

"Fine. Good night, I love you."

"I love you too, honey."

I wake to Josh snoring beside me. I smile at him. All uncertainty has seemed to leave me. I know beyond a shadow of doubt that Camille will return today as my father said. I'm still confused about all of the details, but it's relieving to know Camille should be back soon.

I walk downstairs to find Tiff sitting with an untouched bowl of cereal in front of her. She has her phone in her hands. She keeps touching the screen to refresh it to see if she has a message or missed call from Emmitt. She looks up at me when I enter. She looks like she didn't get a minute of sleep.

"Is it too early to call him?" Tiff asks me.

"No, he'll be awake. Go ahead," I say.

She dials Emmitt. A few seconds pass.

"Emmitt. Is she back?" There's a small pause. "Yes. Oh, that is great news. What? She's disoriented?"

Another small pause, "Okay, we'll see you all at the haunted house."

Tiff hangs up the phone, relieved. She hops up and gives me a hug. "She's back."

"My father said she would be."

"You talked to your father last night?"

"Yes, but only in a dream. I don't know how to travel back and forth, and it sounds like Camille just learned to travel back. She was taken by force. Apparently, we not

66

only have enemies here, but also in my father's world."

"How in the heck are we going to protect you three from that, another world?" Tiff asks.

"My father says he has it under control."

"Not complete control if they were able to take Camille." Tiff gives me a look of desperation.

I am distraught. I'm angry that she's questioning my father's words, but she has a point. I'm going to have to find another window of time to speak with my father.

RETURN

Everyone surrounds Camille when we get to the haunted house. They're asking all sorts of questions and I can tell by the bewildered look she's wearing she doesn't have answers.

"Calm down, everybody. Give the girl a chance to breathe," I say.

Camille gives me a look of appreciation. Emmitt has his big arms around her. In fact, throughout today's final rehearsals he doesn't leave her side unless absolutely necessary. He seems to have to keep touching her by holding hands, putting his arms around her shoulders, or even sitting her in his lap. I think he's afraid she'll disappear again, and he believes that if he's touching her she can't or, if she does, he'll go with her.

"Emmitt, she can't disappear on her own," I say.

"How do you know? Do you know about how I was taken? It was the worst," Camille says.

"I spoke with my father last night. He *died* when I was fourteen. He has different DNA like us. I don't believe he truly died, but now lives in that Other World that you were in."

"What does he look like?"

"He has brown hair and bushy eyebrows. His whole face lights up when he smiles. He has a star tattoo on his shoulder."

"Yes, I saw him. He helped me get back."

"Do you remember the process? Do you think you could repeat it on your own?"

"I do know the process, but I don't intend to ever go back to that world." I can see the look of fear in her eyes. Emmitt's grip on her tightens.

"I would never ask you to do that against your will. I would just like to know for myself. It would be good for Jack to know just in case too. Hopefully, we'll never be forced to use it again, but I feel better being armed and equipped." Josh squeezes my hand as I finish.

"Okay, I can see your point. It's really difficult to explain." Jack leans forward, trying to get as close to Camille as he can so he can learn the process.

"Maybe if you compare it with anything you've experienced before it would help," I offer.

"It's similar to meditation. I focused on where I wanted to go, home. My understanding is that to get to the Other World, one has to be in a state of emergency with high adrenaline. It's the opposite to get back. You have to control your breathing and be as calm as you can be. Meditation helps."

"That doesn't sound too bad," Jack says.

"It sounds easier than it is. When you're in that world everything is different. It's so disorienting that concentrating and keeping calm is almost impossible. If it hadn't been for your father, Austria, I don't think I could have done it."

"He was really good at focusing. I remember him teaching me as a child. Now that I know he was an Olympian, I believe he picked it up in the competitions. Think about being in another country with the world as an audience. You have to be able to focus through it all. Maybe that's why he is so good at it in the Other World."

"How did the person take you from the bathroom to that world?" Brittany asks. I can tell she's disturbed that her friend had been taken from right under her nose. She's popping her neck and her shoulders appear tense.

"He appeared out of nowhere. He was there in the stall with me. Thankfully I had finished and was fully dressed. He popped in with a hand covering my mouth and, before I could react, adrenaline coursed through my body. I had closed my eyes to try to think of an escape. I did escape but didn't recognize anything around me. It was so weird. In the Other World, you feel emotions from everything. Not just people, but plants, streets, anything. It's almost like everything has a visible bubble around it. People have the brightest. When your father first approached me, it was blinding."

"Wow, really? I remember feeling great emotion when I went into a state of shock," I say.

"Can we change the subject? I'm still reassuring myself that I'm really here. It is a somewhat of a downer thinking back to then. Until your father showed up, I had thought I was lost and would never return."

"Yeah, how about everyone grab some dinner before we open for tonight. Camille, are you sure you're up to working? No one would blame you if you wanted to take the night off," Bill says.

"I'm sure. If I don't work, I'll just get lost in thoughts and worries. I'd rather be busy and with everyone around me."

"Well, we have the guards, and you know the check-in schedule. Please adhere to it, everyone."

"No problem," Camille says.

##

Everyone disperses. Each couple goes a different route. Ceresa's by herself and looks a little mystified as to where she should go when Bill side hugs her and asks if she'll join him for dinner. He says he'd like to discuss some of the projects he's working on to help the street kids.

Josh and I walk off with clasped hands. He moves the hair away from my eyes and looks at me. "Where would you like to eat?"

"Have you ever tried Novel? Tiff and I went there once when I first started working for the haunted house, and I've been craving it ever since."

"Sounds perfect to me."

We walk to Novel still holding hands. I still can't seem to drive the thoughts of Camille's kidnapping from my head. If someone took her, why were they not in the Other World with her? Walking in calms me the way it did last time. There are so many questions, but I'm able to set them aside in the comforting surroundings of Novel with my hand in Josh's. Soothing, soft lights and a Tuscan décor cause my muscles to relax instantaneously. Josh puts his arm around me and smiles. I grab a menu as we're waiting to be seated. I explain to him the variety and deliciousness of it. I wonder what his meals have been like growing up.

"What sort of meals did you have growing up?" I dare to ask.

"Pretty dull. I mean I usually had whatever was the cheapest. Fosters had variety.
Once I stayed with an Indian family, and
their food had such a kick, my stomach was
upset the first couple of days. Once I grew
accustomed to it, I enjoyed the flavor."

"What about when you were on the
streets?"

"Canned goods, non-perishables, and
every once in a while a car driving by
would see one of our signs and offer lefto-
vers from whatever restaurant they'd just
had lunch or dinner in. Those were a nice
treat."

"Were you ever starving? Is there anything we could do to help? I know there are
soup kitchens. I have volunteered at one,
but they can't cover all the meals."

"We should've gone with Ceresa and
Bill. They're probably having a very similar conversation."

I wrap my arms around him. "Yeah, but I don't mind being alone with you either."

"Okay, a table has opened up. Follow me, you two," the hostess announces.

We walk to a table toward the back. As we're walking we go by a table of some of my old classmates. This is it. The moment where I stand up for the street kids and do not let this proper yet judging group uproot my feelings.

"How are you? I haven't seen you around lately. What have you been up to?"

"Hey, Monica. I'm good. How are you? Oh yeah, I started a new job and have been really busy."

"Right this way," the hostess says. She must not want us to block the walkway. Novel isn't the biggest restaurant.

I feel like I've lost my chance, but Josh and I are holding hands, so that has to count. Josh and I turn to follow her.

"Can we join you for a bit and catch up? The rest of the group's heading home,"

Dave says as he pulls Monica by her sleeve and steps to follow us.

"Sure," I return.

We all sit down at the table. Josh and I look at the menus. I realize the flaw I've made. I haven't introduced Josh.

"Monica and Dave, this is Josh. We work together at the haunted house. That's my new job."

"A haunted house—that has got to be exciting."

"It is."

I glance at the menu but already know that I want the crab salad with puffed rice, nor, and ginger. There's a lull in conversation. It feels like pulling teeth trying to think of something to say about the haunted house. I could go on and on for hours about it with certain people, but I do not think my old classmates will understand. I look over to Josh to discuss food choices. He appears to be somewhat hiding behind his menu. Does he feel the tension too?

"What's it like to scare people?" Dave asks.

"It's a blast. The employees are artful and talented, and I've been able to put my writing skills to use on scenes. Josh is extremely gifted when it comes to drawing the scenes."

"I bet it's a thrill. So, Josh, are you in costume? That garb you have on would put me on edge in a haunted house," Dave prods.

Josh isn't in costume. He's in the clothes of a street kid. The clothes he always wears.

"No, these are my street clothes. The costumes in the haunted house are epic and would probably make you run if I were in them now," Josh responds.

"Oh, I see," Dave says.

The silence returns. I notice Dave and Monica sizing Josh up. They're just now seeing him for the street kid he is. Then they're looking at me and whispering. Why do they have to be so judgmental? They're going to be talking to all of our classmates, and I'm going to have to explain myself. Why can't they just go?

"Well, we need to be heading off. Everyone's meeting at Tom Fooleries later. You should join us," Dave says.

I notice they don't include Josh in the invite. How rude, but I'm just relieved to have them leaving.

"I'll be working after dinner, but I'll see you guys around," I say.

They get up and walk out. I turn to Josh to help him decide what he'd like from the menu.

"I've heard the Pig Head Pie is to die for, Josh. It comes with asparagus, summer truffle, and comfit lemon."

"I can read the menu, Austria. How come you introduced me to Dave and Monica as your coworker and not your boyfriend? I thought we were beyond the point where you would be ashamed to be with a man from the streets. You were so awkward with them. It was like you were embarrassed to be with me."

"Josh, no. We'd been holding hands. I guess I thought they'd assume the boyfriend part. It was difficult trying to explain the haunted house to them. I just don't think they'd understand this part of my life. Our private school was so rigid and controlled."

"You don't think they'd understand the haunted house part of your life, or dating someone who's from the streets part of your life?"

Josh's face looks broken like he could cry at any second. I guess I really did foul things up. How can I make them better? I'd have us go to Tom Fooleries if we didn't have to work. I'm tongue-tied and don't know what to say.

"Don't worry about it. I'll go back to where my kind belongs. I just thought you were different. My bad."

He gets up before I can reply and storms off. My heart drops to my stomach, and I'm dizzy.

"Josh, wait."

He walks too quickly for me to catch up with him before he exits. The hostess stops me.

"We've scheduled a server for your table. Can you please sit back down and eat?"

Shoot. Well, maybe Josh needs some time to vent. I'm not completely sure how to prove to him that things aren't as he believes. Plus, I need to sit until the dizzy spell ceases. Maybe I need some time to convince myself too. Had I been too embarrassed to introduce him as my boyfriend? What does that say about me?

Dinner's boring by myself, but I'm able to think. Unfortunately, I haven't come up with answers when it's time for me to get back to the haunted house. I don't understand. Josh and I have been through things most people don't face in a lifetime

together. How can he believe that I'm embarrassed by him? Or is there something
going on with him that's more than that?
Have his feelings of inferiority resurfaced
with my different DNA? Great, now things
are going to be weird between me and Josh
again. We're different, with people chasing
us and another world. We don't have time
for this kind of argument. There's a pain in
my side like the stitch you get when you're
running.

ALONE

Walking to the haunted house in a gloomy state, my first destination is the inventory room. Everyone's getting dressed when I head to the costume racks and find the outfit I need. I spot Josh by the vanities. He sees me but looks away without saying a word or waving, or anything. It feels like back when Ed had threatened Josh not to talk to me. Only now, I know this silent treatment is Josh's own decision. That's worse than before. I walk over to Ceresa and Jack to head to our room together. Ceresa gives me a look of disapproval. Josh must have spoken to her about the scene at the restaurant, or at least his version of events. I don't want to misinterpret her. Maybe she's upset about something else.

"Is everything all right, Ceresa?" I ask.

"Don't worry about it. We can keep our distance from you outside of the job if you're embarrassed by us. I'd just allowed myself to believe that, after all we've been through, you would at least respect us."

"It wasn't like that, Ceresa. This whole thing is a misunderstanding. Please don't be upset with me. I do respect you."

"Yeah, whatever."

She walks to the room ahead of us. Jack gives me a confused look.

"Sorry, it looks like Josh talked to the whole group, and a lot of people are upset. I hope you can get this misunderstanding remedied. It feels weird working without people getting along. It feels more like a job when before it just felt like fun," Jack says with a miserable look on his face.

"I know, Jack. I'll do my best. Sorry. Now let's go scare some people."

I'm so furious with how everything has turned into a mess that I look forward to scaring complete strangers. Jack and I sit in the dark corner that will light up when it's time for his "hanging." Ceresa drops to the floor shaking, and Brian shoots himself in the head. I hear gasps from the customers when they believe they're doomed. Jack and I are next. I fit the noose around his neck. I can feel the customers' eyes on us. I kick the chair from beneath him, and he begins to convulse. A customer actually steps to him to help, but Ceresa intervenes. She instructs them to run just as Brian starts after them in his chariot and the lit water illuminates their exit. I'm about to leave so I can check in with the guard and make it to the next room in time when I spot Jack still struggling. He's not acting this time. He really is being hanged, and the convulsions are real. I am lightheaded as I run to him and lift him.

As I'm lifting Jack with one hand and moving the noose off him with the other, shapes appear. They look hazy, like my father did when he conversed with me after I fainted. As Jack is freed I recognize the shapes. It's Matt and Ed. Guess they're still with us when we had thought the haunted house was free of them. Jack slumps down, but now Ceresa has joined him and is caring for his wounds. Matt's shape looks at me and begins talking.

"Looks like your pops isn't the only one who can make physical occurrences happen in this world while being in the other."

So Matt and Ed are like us, the ones with the different DNA. Otherwise, how could they be in the Other World? What do they mean by occurrences?

"What are you talking about?" I ask.

"Oh, you don't remember when your pops busted out all of the haunted house windows trying to warn you there was danger here? Come on, your memory is sharper than that."

"Okay, but what did you do?" I know the answer before they respond. Jack shouldn't have actually hung. The hidden wires should have held him up. The convulsions should've just been merely an act, but they weren't.

Ed gestures toward Jack. Ceresa looks at me like I'm out of my mind. Since she can't see Matt and Ed, she probably believes I am. She doesn't think much of me now anyway. Jack's looking at Matt and Ed fearfully. He's probably coming to the same conclusion I am. We really aren't safe in this world if there are bad guys in the Other World. Apparently, not only can they kidnap us, but they can harm us physically as well. Great, just what we need.

"We just played with the strings that were supposed to hold the kid up. Looks like they're not as effective if loosened a bit," Ed says with a smirk on his face that I wish I could wipe off.

"You wouldn't want to actually harm him though, would you? Your bosses might not be too thrilled to have his organs go to waste now, would they?" I'm mocking

Matt and Ed for making a stupid error. Jack's one of the ones with special DNA. It was foolish of them to put him in danger.

"We knew he'd be saved. Plus that wasn't really what we were after," Matt says.

I'm furious. I wish I could hurt them. Maybe if they're able to make physical occurrences, I can make one happen to them too. The adrenaline almost makes me dizzy as I go in for the attack. I hear Ceresa say, "What in the world?"

I land on a grassy patch near a beach. It's so bright I'm blinded. As my eyes adjust, I look around. A bird trots up a stone stairway. I can feel its excitement. I can feel the grains of sands' love for one another as they cling to each other. A wave hits the beach, and the grains are separated; I feel their longing. I must be in the Other World. One second I had been barreling toward Matt and Ed. The next, I'm in a place I don't recognize even from any dream. I remember Camille mentioning adrenaline having to do with how she moved to this world. So did Matt and Ed take me or did I come of my own free will? I don't see them around, so I hope it was of my own accord. Maybe I'll get back faster because of that. I stand and brush off my costume.

As I begin to walk to the stairs, a bright light makes me shield my eyes. Then I hear his voice. As my eyes adjust again, I recognize the face that goes with the voice. It's my father. He is real. I run up and give him a hug. He hugs me back. I can't stop the tears from flowing down my cheeks. He's really here. I can feel him. He's hugging me back. Again, he smells of the aftershave he used in life.

"Father. So this is where you've been all these years."

"Yes. I've been here watching over you. You won't want to be climbing those stairs just yet."

I step back onto the grass. "Why? What's up there, Father?"

"That's Heaven. We're stuck in a middle world here."

"What? I don't understand any of this."

"Do you feel different than you did at home?"

"Well, everything is different here. I felt the sand grains' emotions." I also feel something different that I hadn't noticed before. I feel dizzy, like I'm about to have a fainting spell, but it isn't bad. It feels like that's the norm in this world. At home, this would feel strange. Here, I feel dizzy, but not bad."

"That's because we are on the Stranded Coil of a Nebula. You see our society is evolving. Some of us ahead of others. One day all of society will live in this world, and we'll all be a step closer to Heaven."

"What about the bad guys? They're here too. Do they get to go to Heaven?"

"I really don't have all of the answers as I'm still here and have not moved on. Since our DNA pulls more energy through the double helix, we have evolved ahead of others. We're within a part of space that will still exist when the Earth no longer does. Because of our DNA, we're able to travel from here to Earth and other places. That's also why you were able to sense shadows and perceptions unlike anyone else, just as I had."

"What? This is intense. There are other places?"

"Yes, but first I need to get you to a safe location. As you know, there are people here who would like to harm us."

"I thought you said you had it under control?"

"I'm sorry, Austria. Their numbers have grown, and I lost control, but we still have something on our side. Let's go to the safe place, and we can discuss it further."

"Okay, Father. What do we do? Do we travel here like on Earth or can we orb somewhere or something?"

He smiles as I say this and takes my hand. "Just walk like you would as if you were on Earth."

"Okay."

I take a step forward, and I swear the sun smiles at me. I take another step forward, and the flowers near the stairway begin to sing. I feel like I'm in a cartoon I saw as a child. I'm walking with my hand in my father's. I've dreamt of holding his hand for years. Is this real? Could it all just be a dream? I think. The wind blows my hair from my face, and I swear I can feel the elation it feels.

"I get to the safe place by thinking about your favorite hiding spot when you were a kid," my father tells me.

"Oh, the hexagon table we had, right?" I can see it perfectly in my head. I close my eyes and remember how I used to open the doors under the table and climb in to hide. When I open my eyes, I see our house in front of me. The blue shutter on the far-right window's still loose as it had been years ago. The daisies are still behind the birdbath to the left of the door. The sweet potato vine drapes over the flower bed to the right of the porch. The door's wide open, and the smell of home-baked cookies wafts out at us.

"Right," my father says with a smile.

HEAVEN

This can't be true. To have things like they used to be. It's what I've dreamt of for many years. Yet, something plagues my heart. My mother isn't here. My haunted house family isn't here. If it weren't for my father beside me, I'd feel as alone as I'd been in that room in the basement where my capturers planned to take my organs. I will enjoy this time with my father, but there are a few things I need to get straight.

"Father, are there others like you or are you all alone?"

"There are others. Come on inside."

We walk inside, and I see a dozen people in our old living room. I don't recognize anyone, but they all offer me warm smiles. An aura makes me feel at home. I follow the scent of cookies and, when I find their tray, I see a face I do recognize.

"Grandmother?"

"Yes, sugar bear, it's me. You didn't think your father got his special DNA from nowhere, did you?" She sets down the tray and gives me a bear hug. "Now eat one of these cookies before they get cold."

I hug her back and then take a cookie. I take a bite. They're delicious as the ones grandmother made me when she was living.

"So we can taste here too?"

"Of course, sugar bear. It's just more in your head now than actual senses. More like waking up memories and triggering your brain the same way they had," my grandmother informs me.

I don't know what to think of all of this, but it feels good, so I take a seat. Sitting on our couch with a pull-out bed as I have dozens of times before gives me comfort.

"We know this must be dreadfully frightening for you," a man I don't recognize states.

"I'm listening with open ears," I reply as I try to prove that I'm here for a purpose, although I'm not sure what that is. I would really like to just spend time with my father and grandmother, but something has to change. We can't continue to be attacked.

"Your grandmother is right. What you experience here is different. A flaw to our foes. You will be able to tell if we're lying or telling the truth as if it were written upon our foreheads," the man states.

"Well, that makes things easier than Earth. It always seems to be a game of poker in my world. You don't get to know others' emotions completely."

"True. I'll begin with history, as that's what I'm most knowledgeable about. I've been here for a long time. Our DNA began evolving as long as a hundred years ago. I'm sure you've guessed that, seeing your grandmother here."

I'm only able to nod; Grandma's definitely not a hundred, but if it began before her, who knows? I don't really want to interrupt this man. The information he is sharing's too valuable.

Fortunately, he continues. "Those with the different DNA also have psychological, physiological, and intellectual aptitudes."

"Well, given my father's Olympic experience and the healing capabilities, I presumed physiological aptitude was involved, but what's this about psychological and intellectual aptitudes?"

"You pick up quick. The psychological is part of the reason you're able to travel here and why your father can communicate with you between worlds. My theory is that with these mental exercises, one's brain grows, increasing intellectual aptitude. So it may not surprise you that, included in our different DNA species, were John Fitzgerald Kennedy, Martin Luther King Jr., and Ronald Reagan."

"Whoa, for real? I have something in common with those guys?"

"Yes you do, as do I. What I'm wondering is if you have put together that they were all either assassinated or experienced attempted assassination."

"Oh, well yeah, I guess so."

"The fight against us has gone on for a long time too."

My grandmother sits beside me and pats my leg. My father is on the arm of the couch and massages my shoulder as if to lighten the load I'm hearing. I hold my grandmother's hand with my right and place my left hand on my father's. "Go on," I say.

"The evil in your world believes that if they can make up the majority of this world, they can gain control. This world's population is much smaller than yours so it would be easier to control this one. When organs are transplanted from someone with our DNA into a normal human in your world, the DNA changes. So by transplanting organs they can move more of their own into this world."

"So that's the true purpose of the human trafficking ring. That's why they're targeting Camille, Jack, and me."

"What you say is true, and we do need to get you, Jack, and Camille prepared. But please let me finish."

"Of course."

"There's a weakness in those with the transplanted special DNA. The ones implanted with the organs aren't able to completely feel emotions here. They can't tell if we lie to them. And they also only get three visits here—"

My father squeezes my shoulder involuntarily. He coughs and interrupts the man, "I don't think we need to dive into that. Let's focus on what has to be done to stop these evil ones."

The man clears his throat and looks my father in his eyes. I feel a sense of apprehension. I know there's something they're withholding but don't know enough to know what it could be.

"Yes, we believe the best way to stop this from happening is to disband their medical research and discontinue the human trafficking," the man continues.

"How are we going to do that? My group has struggled just to keep from being captured and rescuing those of us who have been captured. We can't go to the authorities. Well, except for our restraining orders against Matt and Ed and the arrests made at my rescue. Don't we run the risk of bringing more unwanted attention if we ask for help? There have been bribes passed from our enemies to the authorities," I say.

"All very level-headed questions. We have to do something. They're getting too close. It also appears the ones we don't want to know about us already do, so I don't think we run the risk of bringing more attention to ourselves. That being said, it's still wise to keep this as quiet as we can," the man adds.

I push my fingers across my forehead and then squeeze them over the bridge of my nose. This is all so much to take in at once. My grandmother seems to sense my tension.

"Don't worry, sugar bear. We're going to be with you the entire time you're trying to work things out in your world. I'll even talk to you and give you advice the way your father has been. I was just afraid I'd scare you to death if I did before."

I smile at her. Grandmother always understood. When I was in trouble one day as a child for drawing on the walls, she came into my room when I was in timeout. She explained to me that most children do this when they're young. She said she believed it was just their creativity and understanding of the world blossoming. She also let me know that, unfortunately, doing this caused my parents extra work either by cleaning or having to buy paint. So as adults, we forget what it is to first learn such things and instead focus on the responsibilities at hand. She said as a grandparent looking back she can understand both sides. Finally, she said it would be best if I just tried to focus my creativity in areas that didn't damage my parents' property.

"Thank you, but I don't even know where to begin," I answer and squeeze my grandmother's hand.

"With the medical research. We need to locate anything that points to our DNA. We've already seen which facilities have the information from this world, so we can give you that. We need their research to be corrupted. The human trafficking ring needs legal intervention. We have the locations of the precincts that would be best. They're closest to the houses of internal organ theft. You just need to deliver evidence to their desk and have charges pressed to get the heat on the ones after us. That'll only last so long, though. We were hoping you could work with Bill. He seems to be involved in promoting street-friendly legislation. We would be ever grateful if he could help in this cause too," the man says.

My mind reels back to the street kids. They don't have a home, just as everyone here except me seems to not have an earthly body. This Other World reminds me somewhat of the street kids. Look at how they've all bonded together. I wonder if it's certain shared experiences that cause us to draw together, or if it's things inside of us that cause that. Thinking of the street kids also makes me recall how upset they are with me right now. I find myself massaging my hands out of old habit. It's what helped me when my blood thickened on Earth and what I did to Josh's hands when they tensed in anger. I remember how warm his hand had felt in mine, but that was before. Will I ever feel that warmth again? I wonder if Bill will be interested in helping me.

Maybe I should ask Camille or Jack to approach him instead. I can handle the medical research with the assistance of Luke and Brittany. Even though I'm not wholly confident in this course of action, I'm glad to have a strategy.

"Thank you. It does feel good to have a game plan. This has been an excellent visit. Can I travel back and forth as need be?" I know I'm pushing the envelope here. My father had seemed quite frustrated when the man mentioned this topic with regard to the non-legit DNA individuals, but we don't have time to be withholding information. I mean, I've gone basically my whole teenage life thinking my father was lost to me forever. And here I sit next to him. I feel his hand on my shoulder, which has tightened once more. I smell aftershave. Anything's possible, right?

"Your visits must remain limited. We are only allowed so many," the man states.

My father stands, and his face is red with fury. "Enough. We don't need to worry her with this."

"Father, I have to know!" I say as I stand and now put my hand on his shoulder.

He looks at me with tears in his eyes. "I wish you didn't have to go back. I've missed you so much." He hugs me, and I feel like my heart will break all over again. "But you must live your life,. You must take me out of the equation when pondering your number of visits. Okay?"

"I love you." Looking into his eyes, I could stay in this world forever. I have to blink several times to keep tears from seeping out of my eyes. I do have to get back to Earth because this is bigger than us. We'll be with each other in the end when we walk the stairs. "Please, I have to know."

"You can only come back and be able to return four times. The fifth visit for the true Altered Helixes is the final one. With your fifth visit, you won't be able to return to your world as your body will have fully acclimated to this one. That's also why you're beginning to lose your ability to perceive things on Earth. You're beginning to acclimate to this world already. I didn't know that when I came here the fifth time. I wouldn't have come. I'm sorry I missed your teenage years, baby."

The air's gone from my lungs. I suddenly feel dizzy, as though I could fall. I only get a few more visits with him. He had been taken away from me after all. He didn't want to leave me ever. He loves me. The thought of limited visits triggers a memory from earlier in the conversation. Tension releases from my shoulders.

"Earlier you said the mutant Altered Helixes only get three visits. How many times have Matt and Ed visited?" I say as I try to keep a mischievous smile from my face.

"They've been here twice, but rid that from your head, Austria. You would waste a trip bringing them here for good," my father answers.

"Would they cause the sides to become unbalanced here?" I ask.

"You'd be amazed what you can talk people into when you're able to read their thoughts and they're unable to read yours," the man who had been talking to me earlier states.

My father jabs him in the side playfully, but the look he gives the man clearly says to shut up.

MEMORIES

My father calls a wrap to the meeting. He and my grandmother have set up a dinner for just the three of us. Apparently they've been doing this for some time in hopes that I might one day visit. They've prepared the chicken, asparagus, and brown rice stir-fry that was one of my favorites growing up. Grandmother even has the cloth napkins in the Mickey Mouse rings I used to love. I can't help but feel like a child. If only I could rid myself of the adult worries pressing in on me.

"Remember going to Wonderscope? All three of us went one day when your mother had to work," my father asks, a smile tugging at his mouth.

"I do remember that. They had that room. It was dark, and you'd pose in front of the wall. A light would snap on and then the walls would glow except for where you had been. We played there forever, making puppet shapes with our hands and letter shapes with our bodies," I answer, surprised at how the preschool memories flood back to me.

"I remember you being in awe of the mock spaceship. You lit up at the mention of space. You asked about a hundred questions about how things worked." My father's leaning back in his chair, totally relaxed as he says this.

"You've always been a smart kid. Older children followed your moves in that dark room." The look of endearment my grandmother gives me makes me miss her more than I ever have. A thought strikes me. Grandmother actually did die, or at least I'd thought she had died shortly after Father.

"Grandmother, what happened to you?" I ask, hoping they won't try to hide more from me like they did during the group talk.

"I'd visited this world a few times before. Some of my visits had been with your father. He was in a hurry to try to find answers. He wanted to secure a safer world for you. It had not been so dangerous in my early days. The danger is greater, but we are armed with more intelligence now. Word hadn't gotten around about us then. Your father blames himself because part of what brought us attention was his success in the Olympics. I've told him over and over again that his success had nothing to do with it. Anyhow, I'm showing my age gabbing on like this. When your father made his final visit neither one of us knew that it would be his last. So many of us have tried to stay in your world. It has only been recently as we've witnessed the Stranded Coil becoming overpopulated with Mutated Altered Helixes that we realized our visits were limited. When your father didn't return, I knew something was amiss and travelled back here to see what it was. I quickly learned that I wouldn't be returning to your world either. Can't complain. There's nowhere I would rather be than here with my son."

"Oh. It's been a rough few years for Mother and me."

"Sorry honey," my father says. "We tried and tried to get back, but once you've reached your limit, there's no returning. Although I did figure out how to talk to you when you came of age by conversing with others here."

"So how do you travel back? I don't really want to go. I'm enjoying this time with you more than anything, but we do have to stop the others from overpopulating this world. I want to keep you safe and Mother and my haunted house family safe."

Now my father sits forward in his chair, the relaxation gone. I can see this is the conversation he dreaded, but I'll be back a few more times, and I'll be sure at least one is quality time. It almost feels like I'm not really going to be leaving him since we can still communicate in my world. Is there really more to life than the conversations we have together whether they be spoken, written, or in body language? It has always been what's set us apart from other species on Earth. It's why the technological age has grown so quickly. Instant conversation via texts to close contacts or to the masses via social media, we cling to it because it's part of our essential being.

"Are you sure you're ready? We could spend some more time here, honey. You could hang with Grams and I."

"Father, I have to stop the medical research and human trafficking. Plus how quickly does time pass in my world compared to this one?"

"Well, more time passes here than on Earth. So when you return it will seem to those in your world as if you've only been gone minutes. The Stranded Coil cause this world to somewhat pause in time like a black hole. Some of those here with scientific backgrounds say the time's speeding up with the population of the mutated helixes."

"Well, I guess I could wait a little bit."

They get up and gesture for me to follow. We walk out the back door and, to my amazement, the tire swing from my childhood still hangs from the oak tree just as on Earth. I run to it in glee. I climb in and smile at my father and grandmother. Their faces light up. My father pushes me until I reach a decent height. I lean back and begin pumping my legs. The warm breeze that washes over me makes me forget my worries. I could stay here in the shelter of my father and leave all my frets behind. Josh and half my haunted house family don't care about me anyway. Tiff would understand. She's had to hold me too many times as I sobbed over my father not being able to see me grow up. I could get a note to my mother so she would know what happened to me.

As I slow down, their faces wash through my thoughts. Little Jack and Lea. They'd be torn apart if Jack were seized by the human traffickers. Emmitt, Brittany, and Landon would lose their apartment and be heartbroken if Camille were taken. Tiff, my best friend, is like a sister. If I don't return, she'll crumble like I did when I lost my father. My mother would do everything within her power to get to me, including putting herself in danger. Luke, Ceresa, Ethan, and Patrice have become family to me. They might be mad at me, but I have to believe they'll forgive me. Just the thought of Josh makes my heart skip a beat, and I drop from the tire swing. Could he forgive me? I have to give it a shot.

Thankfully, my grandmother and father both seem to comprehend the thoughts going through my head. They give me a hug and then each take one of my hands. Then they take each other's hands, forming a circle.

"You have to relax and slow your breathing," my grandmother says. Her voice soothes me into a serene state. Then memories flood back of how I'd done this on my own when I first saw the shadows at the haunted house, calming myself down with breathing and other techniques. Had I been escaping travelling to this world by calming my reactions down before? When had I stopped doing that? Once my father began visiting me? When I realized he was one of the shadows? Is that why I'd been able to see Matt and Ed, or had they visited me the way my father had? Is that why I'd finally been able to allow adrenaline to take over and travel here? There are so many questions.

I must calm down in order to travel back. "Remember how Mother always makes home-made chicken noodle soup whenever one of us is sick?" I ask my father and grandmother.

They both look at me and smile. They squeeze my hands. Mother always has a way of making me feel safe. Then I remember Josh offering to make me tea. I begin to swirl or at least that's what it feels like. It reminds me of Dorothy's flight to Oz, except this one is full of happy memories. Maybe this is like her flight back to Kansas. "There's no place like home," I whisper and open my eyes.

##

"Whoa. Now that there is just trippy." It sounds like Ceresa's voice.

"Where, where am I?" I ask as I blink my eyes against the bright lights.

"You're in the inventory room. We closed the haunted house early, kid. Jack needed to rest, and you'd disappeared. We couldn't go on without you two," Bill informs me.

"What happened?" Tiff's sitting at my hips as I lie on the floor of the inventory room.

"I, well, do I have to explain here?"

"Yes." I hadn't noticed Josh sitting on my left side. He looks deeply disturbed. I wonder what he thinks.

"I'm so sorry, Josh. I really didn't mean to not claim you as my boyfriend at the restaurant. Things were just so awkward. I didn't handle myself the way I wanted to. Please forgive me." His face looks stunned as if he hadn't seen this coming.

"Oh, who cares about that? Even new street kids themselves get tongue-tied trying to explain their fresh bonds to old ones. Plus, Josh was trying to find a way to protect you. His acting upset was a hoax in order to achieve separation from you so he could get a plan together behind your back," Ceresa pats my shoulder in reassurance. "What in the hell were you doing? First you saved Jack from being hung. I'm still uncertain as to how that happened. Then you were yelling at nothing. When you tried to tackle that same nothing, you vanished in thin air. I've seen a lot of creepy things in my time, but that beats them all."

"I travelled to the Other World," I whisper as I look around to ascertain my audience. Josh is to the left, near my face, with Ethan and Patrice behind him. Ceresa's to my right with Landon and Brittany behind her. Luke and Tiff are by my hips on either side. Jack and Lea are at my left foot. Jack looks tired, but he also has a look of awe. Camille and Emmitt are at my right foot, and Camille's jaw has dropped. I take another look at Josh and smile. So he wasn't upset with me; it had all been a setup so he could protect me.

"So you figured out how to travel there on your own?" Camille asks.

That's when Bill interrupts. I'd forgotten about him standing behind my head.

"What on Earth are you kids talking about?"

ADAPTION

I begin explaining the Other World. Bill knows about the different DNA and that Camille disappeared. When I tell them about my visit with my father and grand-mother, everyone's face is focused on mine.

"You were right about the blinding light, Camille. I wasn't even able to adjust my eyes when my father first appeared. Did you visit any places from your past?"

"I was too freaked out. Maybe since I don't have relatives there, I don't have any old places there either. Plus, I could only concentrate on your father's explanation of how to return."

"It does help having people you care about there, but I believe that world feeds off of your memories and emotions and produces what you want a little too."

The faces around me help me recollect what I want. I need them to be safe. Jack, my pseudo little brother, cannot live his life in fear. Camille, the one who's spoken to my father, can't run forever. I have to get a plan into action.

"My grandmother and father shared some vital information." Everyone had brought chairs and boxes over to sit around me while I talk. Josh brings me a chair and helps me into it. I grab his hand and hold it firmly. I need him now more than ever. I see Bill has taken out a notebook and pen.

"The ones after the different DNA are primarily two groups. They have people in the human trafficking industry that we're well aware of. They also have people in medical research. When an organ from a body with different DNA is implanted into a regular (normal DNA) host, the host's DNA is changed too, but not completely.

For example, Ed and Matt were not born with different DNA; they only have Mutated Altered Helixes. They're only able to travel to the Other World three times. On their third visit, they're stuck there and cannot return to our world."

"Wait, what? So how many times can we travel and why is it limited?" a worried Camille asks.

"We can travel five times, but our fifth is our last as our bodies fully acclimate to that world."

"Whoa," Jack comments.

"And how many times have Matt and Ed travelled?" Ceresa asks with a smirk upon her face.

"They've travelled to the Other World twice. Their next travel will be their last."

"Nice," Ceresa says.

"Do your grandmother and father have a plan for how to deal with the human trafficking and medical research?" Bill wisely asks. I'm grateful as he helps me stay on track. The enthusiasm in Ceresa's questions about Matt and Ed had diverted my attention.

"Yes, Bill, with the help of their group in the Other World, there's a plan. We need to corrupt the medical research. We can prohibit the medical research and human trafficking by having legislation put into place. Bill, I'm going to need your help with that. Corrupting the research will keep it from growing after it's been stopped. We want it to appear that the findings of different DNA were a mistake, so no other scientists are drawn to research it. We also need to bring charges against the human trafficking. We have the charges from our abductions and restraining orders, but it would be good to get more of their group behind bars. I'd like to have more damaging evidence when we do."

"What do you mean you need Bill's help with legislation? Don't we have enough to worry about with the homes for children bills we're trying to have passed?" Ceresa asks, letting out a sigh of disappointment.

"The bills you have in action for the homes for children will pass with ease with the help of my father and grandmother. You'd be surprised at how persuasive a spirit from another world can be to a politician. They just need you to draft the bills."

"Interesting. I'll have to see what I can do. I wish I could discuss it with your father and grandmother," Bill responds.

"How do you plan on corrupting the medical research?" Luke asks. With his medical schooling, it seems this topic has piqued his interest.

"We know the locations of the medical research involved with studies of the different DNA. One being Dr. Shipley, who informed the human traffickers of both Jack's and my different DNA. I'm still not entirely sure how they know about yours. Camille. What doctor do you go to?"

"I see Dr. Pike, but I've seen him since I was a kid. He's a sweet old man. I don't think he'd be involved in something like this," Camille says.

"You're probably right, but let's take a look just in case. We should probably have a look at the blood donation center too," I say.

"Do you mind if I take a sample of your blood to study so I can see what will be in the medical research we're looking for?" Luke's mindset is already as if he were wearing scrubs.

Uh, another vial. "Sure, no problem." Have to do what I have to do.

"Thank you. I have an idea of how to corrupt the research. You said Dr. Shipley mentioned the 95% of DNA that used to be viewed as meaningless, right?"

"Yes." Hope sparks within me. I'm so glad we have Luke on board and that he isn't as self-serving as his fraternity counterparts, Matt and Ed.

"Much of the DNA being tested now is showing marks and signs of diseases such as cancer. If I can manipulate the different DNA to mirror this, the research will be thrown into disease studies. There's so much data on that, it should be hidden within piles of other research. And, if it's found, I can also show foreign matter within the findings, rendering them for the most part useless. We can't just delete them completely because that would be easily detected."

"That sounds perfect, Luke," Tiff says as she grabs his arm and holds it.

"So it seems we have a plan for the medical research. Now, how do you plan on getting more evidence against the human traffickers?" Bill asks.

Josh's hand tightens on mine as Bill finishes.

"My father and grandmother have those locations too, but we can't really go into police headquarters claiming we know the locations because some spirits told us, now can we? I'd like to have surveillance set up at the locations. I think if we can get photographs of those involved at the sites and evidence of human trafficking activity, we can get most of these places shut down and the perpetrators behind bars. I'd like to make these reports at the same time as we corrupt the medical research, so we'll have to work quickly."

"There has to be a head. I mean all groups like this have leaders, don't they? We should find out who that is and present evidence that incriminates them," Ethan adds. I find myself smiling at his sharp thinking.

Josh stands then, letting go of my hand. "No, we're putting ourselves in way too much danger. How are we to stop a group that's been at this for years? Austria, get that smile off your face. You will most definitely not be involved. What do you intend to do? Walk up to the headperson's house and ask for a fingerprint?"

"I don't want anyone in danger, Josh. We'll find a way to collect evidence without them knowing we're doing so," I say and put my hands around his head and begin peck kissing him all over his face. "Please?" I repeat over and over with each kiss.

He grabs me and tries to push me away, but I jump up on him so that if he doesn't catch me, we'll both fall. As he holds me, I feel like everything is going to be okay. I kiss him one last time. "Everything's going to be fine, Josh."

He shakes his head and then kisses me back.

"Get a room, you two," Ceresa complains.

HEIST

Luke looks ridiculous in his costume of camouflage. He has black and green makeup all over his face. His white teeth stand out when he smiles at me. Josh looks just as ridiculous. His eyes are even more prominent now, like an owl in the dark. Tiff has dark pants, a dark long-sleeve shirt, and dark gloves on. We all look like we're getting ready to rob a bank. Brittany has her dirty blonde hair hidden beneath a dark green stocking cap. We're getting ready to go to the first location of medical research. I'm excited to finally be making an offensive move, rather than just defending.

As we park a block away from the medical building, I look out to make sure we haven't been seen. We appear to be undetected. We're close to the alley that leads up to the building. As we enter the alley, a shadow flies by me. Great, right now I don't know if the shadow is from a good or bad helix, but I'm sure it's one. If it were my father, wouldn't he talk to me? I'm going to have to be very careful as we go about this venture.

Josh picks the lock like a pro. Guess when you're stuck between living on the streets and finding a place to stay warm, you acquire a few talents. Luke enters first, shining a flashlight around to see if there are any occupants. Tiff follows him when he gives us a thumbs-up, meaning it's all clear. Josh gestures for Brittany to follow them and then grabs my hand as we bring up the rear. Luke's entering the code into the alarm system my father had seen while spying as a shadow. I'm filled with relief when it's inactivated. He then goes to the computer. We have the login information from my father too. My father had informed us the software used is from

Descry, a large local global supplier of healthcare information technology. Luke has trained on this exact technology at medical school.

Ironic that the software we're using is called the Helix Flat File. As Luke begins manipulating the data to make it look like disease research, he tells us where the specimens are stored. Tiff stays with Luke as Brittany, Josh, and I go to the specified refrigerated storage. We each have multiple needles to stick through the rubber stoppers and insert the foreign data. It seems like an hour has passed by the time we're done. I'm anxious to get out of here. Josh blinks his own flashlight in Luke's direction three times to let him know our part of the mission is complete. Luke will now add the foreign data findings to the Altered Helix disease research data. He blinks his flashlight three times at us to let us know he's finished.

Luke keeps his flashlight pointed toward us as we make our way back to Tiff and him.

"Whoa, I found something interesting I think we can use," Luke exclaims as we make our way.

We're almost to them when I see the shadow dart by. I become overwhelmed with a feeling of anger. Brittany's in front of me and Josh behind me. That's when I notice Matt and Ed's features behind the metal filing cabinet. They're not hazy this time. They're here in real life. How did they know where to find us and when? I gasp a breath in. Who was the shadow then? Was someone from the Other World trying to warn us? Josh must've seen my reaction and that I'm looking directly above the cabinet. He must see Matt and Ed because he pushes me and Brittany out of harm's way just as I see Matt and Ed push the cabinet. It catches Josh on the shoulder and takes him down. His arm is caught under it. I take one look at him. Luke's already removing the cabinet. He must have started heading our direction before the push. I wonder if he saw Matt and Ed too. I'm a little surprised they didn't go after him. Why would they want to harm my body? The game's changing. They must have found more Altered Helixes than I'd thought for my body to be so useless. They know I'm coming after them. Yes, the game certainly has changed.

"Are you okay?" I ask Josh.

"Yes, but Austria…" Josh pleads.

I don't wait for him to continue. I'm attacking Matt and Ed before another word can come out. Ceresa will be pleased when she hears that I'm taking them to the Other World for good.

As the adrenaline rushes through my veins, I make sure to grab both of their arms. They try to escape my grip, but I just let my fingernails dig deeper into their skin. I focus on the image of Josh caught beneath the cabinet as I let the adrenaline take over. This time, when I land on the grassy patch near the ocean, I'm tangled with Matt and Ed. Matt punches me in the side. Ouch, I had hoped I wouldn't feel pain here. I wonder if I actually do or if it's just a psychological reaction. Ed kicks me off him.

I'm about to kick and punch back when Matt and Ed are taken away by many hands. My father, the man who spoke so much at my house in this world last time, and a couple of somewhat familiar guys have restrained Matt and Ed.

"Take them to the barn. These here are our captives. Maybe if they share some information with us, they can go free," the man who spoke to me at the house says.

"Yeah, right, like we're going to tell you anything," exclaims Matt.

One of the somewhat familiar guys punches him right in the belly. "I think we should gut them like they've done to some of us."

"No more talking. Just have them re-strained at the barn and set up guard duty," my father interjects.

I rub my side and stare at them as they're carted off. Something feels wrong, like we're now the bad guys. I guess we can get good intelligence from them, but as much as I dislike the pair, my stomach twists at the thought of them being gutted. I know they wouldn't hesitate to do that to me, but I don't want to stoop to their level.

Once they're out of sight, my father approaches me. "You okay, kid?"

"Yeah, I'm fine."

He must've noticed the look of reproach I had as Matt and Ed were hauled off. "You know they're not really going to gut them. Matt and Ed just can't tell a lie here, so we're going to be able to get information out of them without harming them. Plus as you now see, even what seems like physical action does no harm."

My pain seems to disappear just as he says the words. It must truly be a psychological reaction.

"Is Josh okay? I have to get back. I have no clue what's going on down there. They pushed a cabinet on him."

"He's fine. Your team has done marvelously. You all successfully took down one medical research location. The other team, with what's his name, Ethan I think, found the other human trafficking site. They're working on getting more surveillance as we speak. Today I was able to help the homes for children legislation move forward. Bill and Ceresa are on board with helping impose laws against our enemies now. The day has been good."

"Oh, wow." I walk over to my father and give him a hug. There has been so much going on. Before I know it, he's carrying me, and he's walking. When we make it to the house, he lays me on the couch and covers me with a blanket. I fall asleep to him kissing my forehead.

Dreams in this world are different. Memories spin into premonitions and hopes spin into recollections. I see my father walking with me on his shoulders as we head to the Liberty Memorial; then he's being chased, and I'm nowhere in sight. I watch from behind a hedge. He must have hidden me to protect me, but to watch him being taken away from me is worse. I take a step to run after his pursuers when a hand touches my shoulder. I look to see who the hand belongs to and find my grandmother.

"You have to let him go, child. All he wants is for you to have a life. You'll understand one day when you have children of your own. It's harder for me to stay here, trust me, but he asked for one last favor before I go. That was to protect you, and I mean to do so."

"I don't understand." My body trembles as I respond.

"There, there. It's going to be fine."

I wake and look around. My father sits safely in the recliner next to me. That was so weird—it felt real. I know our thoughts are different in this world. Was my grandmother trying to send me a message of some sort? If so, I have to stop whatever it is that will cause my father to put himself in danger before it happens.

"You all rested up, kid?" my father asks me. His hair is all askew from sleep. He looks older, as if the stress of everything going on has aged him. I wonder if people age in this world. If it weren't for the bags below his eyes, I'd swear he had not aged a day since I last saw him alive in my world.

"Yeah I slept, but I still feel anxious. Are you guys going to be okay here while we work in my world? Will they come after you knowing you have Matt and Ed?"

"No need to worry. Matt and Ed are pretty low in their chain of command. I don't really see much action being taken."

"Are you sure? I thought their parents were involved in the human trafficking and have financial pull on Earth. It's not like you have police and hospitals you can go to here."

"We have each other, the Altered Helixes, and that's enough."

"Okay, so what's the plan now?"

"I think it's best to continue with the original plan. You have to get back, honey."

"I know, but I've been here two times now. I only have two more visits until my final one."

"I'll always be with you. I'll always look after you." A shiver causes my joints to jerk as he says this. He knows. He knows he's going to be in danger, and he wants me away from him, so I don't have to see it. He's preparing me. What can I do though? I have to keep the others safe.

"So what will you do here while we're working down there? You already have helped with the homes for children laws and now have Matt and Ed in custody."

"We're going to continue to run interference in case any of you get into trouble during your missions."

"Won't that put you in jeopardy?"

"We've been here watching them for years. We have a plan. Now you need to return before you worry everyone back home."

He's avoiding my questions. What can I do? I can't force it out of him. He's probably already aware that I'm feeling things out. I'll just have to think on it and hope to come up with something before it's too late.

"Okay, can I swing on the tire again?"

He smiles and musses my hair. When he stands, so do I. His broad shoulders seem to carry the weight of the world. He smiles as he gets the swing started. That smile makes memories rush through my head as I pump my legs.

CRASH

I wake in my own bed. Josh is lying next to me, cradling a pillow as if it can fill the emptiness. In the moonlight from the window, I see how puffy the skin around his eyes is. My eyes widen as I see what's propped on the pillow. His arm is in a blue cast. Everyone has signed it. I climb out of my bed to grab a sharpie from my desk. "To my love, I vow always to protect you from this or any world. –Austria." He begins to stir as I put the cap back on the marker. His eyes flutter as they adjust to the darkness.

"Who are you? What do you want?" His muscles are flexed, and he's searching for an object. I have to speak before he finds one and hits me over the head with it.

"Josh, it's me. You're safe." I hate that they've caused fear to invade his life again.

"How did you get here? Did you take Matt and Ed to the Other World?"

"I got back the same as last time. I'm not sure why I'm here, but I think it must have been because I had just awoken there. Yes, Matt and Ed will not be returning to this world."

His breathing slows, and I can see his muscles relax again. "That's good. I don't mind never having to see those two again."

"Are you okay? Is anything else besides your arm hurt?" I touch his cast and have to roll my shoulders to release the tension.

"Na, just the arm. I have a couple scrapes and bruises, but they're nothing."

"Were we successful with the medical research facility? It had seemed as though we were, but I remember Luke saying he'd found something interesting. What was it?"

"Let's wake up Luke and Tiff and discuss it together. Part of my memory of that trip seems to be incomplete. I think I

suffered a minor concussion when the filing cabinet fell on me."

Those jerks caused him another concussion. Now part of me hopes my father's
group *will* gut them. Who am I kidding, the
very thought of that upsets my entire being.

"Oh, Josh, I'm so sorry. Are you going
to be okay?"

"Yeah, nothing I haven't been through
before. Please don't worry about it."

"Okay. What time is it?" I move in to
give him a hug. It's awkward with the cast
but warm at the same time.

"It's seven in the morning. They'll be
up soon enough. Can we hang out here, just
the two of us for a while?"

We lay down side by side with the cast
propped on my hip. I've always gotten lost
looking into his eyes. I find myself losing
time and worry. He smiles at me with his
beautiful smile and eyelashes touching his
cheeks. Then his emotions seem to shift as
he reads his cast.

"From this world or ANY world…really, Austria. I don't want you going back to the Other World. What if they figure out how many visits you have left and just take you without your consent, and you end up stuck there?"

"I will only go for important reasons. It's nice to see my father, but he wants me to live a normal life. Plus, now we don't have to worry about Matt and Ed."

"But aren't they able to cause physical things to happen here while they're in that world?"

"Yes, but not when they're in my father's custody."

"Whoa. Okay, but please be careful."

"Okay."

We kiss, and the seconds fly by. I wish I could just spend eternity in this electrical outburst. It feels as though my heart will explode through my chest. I grab his shirt. He runs his fingers through my hair. I hear footsteps approaching the door.

"Josh, are you okay? I thought I heard voices in there," Tiff asks from outside the door.

Shoot, the kiss has to end.

"I'm fine, Tiff. Austria's back."

She's opening the door before we can move out of our embrace. She jumps on the bed and grabs me. I see an agonizing look cross Josh's face as she lands. The arm must give him worse pain than he let on. She's hugging me from behind, and I can feel her smile through her cheek on the side of my head.

"I knew you'd come back."

"What? Did some people believe I wouldn't?"

"Well, I know how much you've missed your father. We always wonder if you won't stay there with him sometime."

"And miss out on all the fun here? Never."

I hug her back with my arm behind me.

Luke enters but seems disoriented. "I need some coffee. I don't know how you girls just pop out of bed full of energy."

Tiff gets up and wraps her arms around him. "And I don't know how you pull all-nighters studying for med school."

"I'll get the pot brewing," I say.

I get up and throw on a robe. I'm not sure how I got into my pajamas as I went into the Other World fully clothed. Josh slowly gets out of bed and holds my hand with his good arm.

"I'll help," he says, though I'm not sure how much help he can be with only one arm working. Not that I'm going to turn him down. I want to spend as much time with him as I can.

I scoop coffee as he one-handedly puts the filter in its place. The aroma as it brews awakens my memory of our strategy. I need to know everything that's happened and what our next steps should be. What methods need revising or reorganizing? If they

146

knew we'd be at the medical research facility, how much more of our blueprint do they have? Did the others encounter interference like we did?

"So, Luke, before I disappeared I remember you saying that you'd found something interesting. What was it?"

He sits down, and I hand him a mug of coffee. He takes a sip before answering. "Yes, I did. We were successful in changing and corrupting the research, but I also stumbled upon some research I wasn't expecting to find. Apparently, they don't want their enemies to be interested in stealing their organs. Kind of ironic since they're so interested in stealing others' organs. They implanted organs from a copycat DNA individual into a test host. They probably kidnapped both of these individuals to be used in the research like lab rats. Anyway, the implanted organs altered DNA again. So, as a defense maneuver, they're developing a serum to protect themselves. Unfortunately for them, so far the serum is only effective on natural-born Altered Helixes."

"Whoa. Nice find. So does that mean Camille, Jack, and I could take this serum, and our organs would become useless to them?"

"That's precisely what it means. Pretty nice for them to do all that work for us. I need to conduct research to see how they would know you've been injected with the serum. Not really useful to us if they still take your organs and they fail on the implanted subject. I need to see if tests have to be run for them to see, or if there's another indicator. They had to have set something up to deter their enemies."

"Or maybe they just want to keep their enemies out of the Other World so they can rule. Whatever you do, be sure to take precautions," I say.

This new development is key. We may not have to target human trafficking through legislation and surveillance if they no longer have reason to steal our organs. A thought comes to mind. They do all of their research via the Helix Flat File. If we could update the data to show we've been vaccinated by the serum, maybe that would stop them from targeting us. I see the problem with this course of action immediately. Once we update the file with this data, they will know. They will surely know that we're tampering with their work. They'll know we are administering the serum to natural born Altered Helixes. This could work, but we'll have to wait to update the file until our mission's complete. We still need the legislation, medical research corruption, and surveillance until we've administered all the serum we can.

"There's one thing I would like to do before we continue on our missions," Josh says and then calmly sips his coffee while sitting at the table. He looks at Luke and

Tiff, and I instantly feel the tension. What now?

"Yes, Josh, what is it?" I ask.

"I want you and Jack to learn some self-defense like Camille. She was able to elbow that man who tried to chloroform her. If there are forms of defense to be learned in the Other World, I would like you all to learn those too. Even though I'd rather you never go back there."

"I can do that. Cheer up, Josh. We're working to bring this all to an end."

He takes another sip and looks at Luke and Tiff. He then stares at the table like there's a whole book written on it. What's going on?

ELABORATION

At the haunted house, Ethan informs us of their success at the human trafficking location.

So far, we've been quite successful. We're sure to be triumphant if everything else goes this smoothly, but I have a foreboding feeling that a bad experience is lurking around the corner.

"The surveillance was boring at first. Just sitting in a car waiting for action to happen. They actually brought in an Altered Helix while we were there. This couldn't be a coincidence. They must be bringing in people daily. Anyway, we called the cops anonymously from the untraceable TracFone and then removed the battery and SIM card. We were down the street when the cops arrived and saw them remove multiple people in handcuffs. Unfortunately, we also saw a gurney roll out with a black bag on top. There had to be a body inside."

Well, at least more of them are detained. The thought of the body inside the black bag makes my blood thicken, and my hands and feet begin to tingle. I have to figure out why my Altered Helix also causes these side effects. Self-defense training will be no good if I die of a heart attack in the heat of the moment. I wonder if it's part of the acclimation process. I'm glad Ethan was smart enough to remove the battery from the phone. Since the cops have been receiving payoffs from our enemies, they could track us through e-911 searches. I'm upset that Ethan was unable to find the leader of that location. Did he even try?

"So who was the leader?" I ask, not particularly hiding my irritation but also not wanting to cause a confrontation.

"We didn't get that. We were hoping to save the person they had, but I guess we were too late for that."

"They're going to know we're tailing them with the call in," I say.

"Oh, lay off, Austria. We have more of them detained," Patrice says as she coddles Ethan.

I'm furious, but I can't turn them against me now. I'm tired of having to prove myself to people. Having to make them be on my side. Do they not understand how vital this is?

Camille answers as if she can read my thoughts. "We did get bugs on those detained. We've been recording their conversations."

"You what? How in the world? Do I even want to know?"

"It just so happens a buddy of ours is a prison employee. He's responsible for checking in inmates," Camille speaks again.

"And how does that help us?" I ask.

"He hid microscopic bugs I preemptively provided him on their clothes."

"You what? How does that work?"

"Well, these will only work until the clothes are washed, but they'll pick up all of the phone calls made within the first twenty-four hours. I think we have the leader you're looking for."

She pulls out her smartphone and opens an app I'm unfamiliar with. When the audio begins, I'm taken aback by the blatant name usage and detail given. I would think they'd be more cautious when making a phone call from jail. Wouldn't the police be scanning those? Oh wait, the payoffs. There must be payoffs to prison guards and employees as well. So this must not be the first time they've been caught in action. Maybe I had been wrong to assume they would think it was us.

"That's great, guys. I'm sorry I was upset earlier. You guys deserve props for doing what you did."

"Did you hear who they named as the lead person?" Patrice asks with a look of astonishment.

I'm really surprised that anything I do can astonish her at this point. She must have taken my questioning more personally than I realized.

"Yes, Patrice, I heard. It just doesn't come as too much of a shock for me is all. I really should have seen it before. I'm pretty upset with myself for that," I say as I wonder why my strong Perceptions didn't give me more of a clue.

"So you're saying that you believe Adam, the Edge of Hell owner and the one revitalizing abandoned buildings, is the leader?" Bill asks from the other side of the room. I can see by his expression that he's taken aback. Of course, he didn't want to work alongside Adam because of the drug usage, but I don't think he'd ever considered his onetime friend to be going down the road of leading a ring involved with the organ theft in this area.

"Don't take it personally, Bill. The group doing this is trying to get complete control of the Other World. They're more influential and threatening than we give them credit for," I say, trying to soothe his hurt ego. I mean, this guy has been his friend for years.

"Thanks, Austria." I see his recoiling even though no one else does. He's going to distance himself from us. We've pushed him to his limit. He's not going to be able to believe all of this if it means accepting that someone who was once almost a brother to him is the worst villain alive. I have to get him off this train of thought. We still need him to get the legislation against human trafficking rolling.

"Bill, you've housed those without homes for years. They're your family. I believe the Altered Helixes among them are the ones in greatest danger. I mean, most of them don't have contacts that will readily notice them missing, so this group runs less risk kidnapping them and taking their organs than they do with individuals who have a residence and steady way of living."

"Really, you still gotta throw your biases up in the air," Ceresa claims.

"These are not biases. It's a fact that a person without a home can go missing and be much more likely to never be searched for than an individual living with a family of five or a businesswoman with meetings filling her day."

"Whatever. The street family is a close-knit group. We all know each other and everyone's habits. I think some of you people with homes become more solitary than us."

"Okay. Well, either way, we can't just start administering the serum. When we do administer the serum, we're going to be broadcasting that it has been done so our enemies will lose the desire to kidnap Altered Helixes. We won't be able to administer it to every Altered Helix at the same time. We need to continue with the legislation, medical research corruption, and surveillance until we've administered as much serum as we can."

"We'll work on the legislation. It's all I can do to make up for the fact that Adam is involved. I should've stayed in better touch with him. Ceresa, I know you're upset about this taking away attention from helping the street kids, but Austria's father really got our legislation for the homes for children going. You owe them too. And, biases aside, without shelter, those without homes are vulnerable. This has to be stopped."

"Thanks, Bill," I exclaim.

"Yeah, yeah. Fine, I'm in." Ceresa pouts.

"Camille, where did you learn self-defense?" Josh asks.

"Just down the street. Some of my college buddies started a gym solely focused on it. Emmitt and Landon have helped me and Brittany train. You don't want to be sleeping on the streets defenseless."

"I think we all could use some training before going out again," Josh says as he tilts his head sideways and looks at me.

"Can I train with Josh first? I want to learn how hard to jab my elbow into his side if he grabs me." I put my arms around his neck and smile.

"This is serious. We all need this training. We're diving deeper into danger. All of us need to be prepared and take precautions." Josh puts his forehead against mine and holds my forearm.

TRAINING

It is not fun being punched in the face. I feel as though this feud is being way overdone, but in order to best prepare to defend ourselves when necessary, Emmitt claims this is imperative. I don't care if it's by a glove padded fist. It is painful. I thought self-defense training was going to be different than this. Emmitt hits me again. I guess I was paired with him because of my height, but he's more built than I'll ever be. This is unfair. Wait, I see an opening. Every time he punches me, he leans to the left first. This time when he leans, I move in the same direction he does. He thinks he's going to knock me out this time, but I quickly lean the other way and jab him in the ribs.

"Ouch." He holds his side. "Good job, Austria, you're now seeing weak spots in your opponent rather than focusing on just protecting yourself. We do need to work on that, though."

"Can we work on it without you punching me in the face?"

"Yeah, everybody head over to the red mats," Emmitt announces to us all.

Jack's face looks swollen. Landon isn't much bigger than him, but he's had much more fighting experience. I don't even want to see what my face looks like. Jack looks frustrated and furious. I feel the same. On the red mats are wood planks balanced on cinderblocks.

"What are these for? Don't we have enough injuries for one day?" I ask.

"You'll be amazed at what we can do with these," Camille says. "Have either of you tested your strength since you found out you had different DNA? I used to think I could break these because I'd practiced, but now I'm not so sure. Let's see how you do."

Jack and I look at each other and nod our heads side to side. They can't be serious. We're going to break our hands.

"Once you witness your own strength, I bet your fighting will change too," Landon inputs.

Jack and I each stand in front of a set of wooden planks. I take a deep breath in and try to focus. Landon stands on the other side of my planks in front of me. He shows me the stance I need to take and the way I should strike. I try to mimic him with a practice swing.

"Are you in pain?" Landon asks me.

"What do you think?" I say with a snarl.

"Use that anger to break the planks. Imagine the wood is Emmitt's face."

"Man, I heard that," Emmitt exclaims.

"Go back to training, Jack," Landon replies.

I think about the shock of Emmitt's first punch. I think about the scar on my abdomen. I think about my father being forced to be away from me too early. Dots begin to circle my vision of the wood. I breathe in again. I can see the grain of the wood very clearly. I can smell the pine. I squeeze my eyes shut in fear of splinters and use all the force I can to send my fist into the wood. I hope I don't break a bone. A flash of light seems to gleam from the wood as I hit it. As I stand from the squat I went into while hitting the wood, I see in the mirror behind Landon what I did. I can't believe it. Waves of emotion rush through me. I can do this. I am strong. I just broke three wood planks with my fist. I look down at my knuckles to see if there's blood. Landon puts his hand on my shoulder. I look up at him, and I can tell he's talking, but I don't hear a thing. I smile, walk to the bench, and sit down.

That's when I look at Jack. He has just broken three planks too. His eyes are huge.

He looks up at me, and I pat the bench next to me. Emmitt, Landon, Camille, and Josh are all staring at the wooden splinters on the floor in amazement.

"Guess, I'm not the only Hercules around here now, huh," Camille says as she nudges Emmitt and smiles. My hearing has returned.

Jack still hasn't said a word. He keeps inspecting his hands as if he's going to find something different.

"What was that?" he asks me.

"I don't know. I've never done anything like that before, but there has been all this talk about how this DNA is supposed to make us stronger and able to heal faster. My father was an Olympian. I guess I just never really believed it would happen to me."

"I know what you mean," he replies.

"Well, let's go see what else we can do."

We both stand and return to the group. They all look at us like we're different people than we were five minutes ago.

"Quit looking at me like that, Josh, or I'll begin self-defense lessons on you." I playfully pinch his side.

"Uh, just surprised is all. I've never been against a woman who topped me." He puts his arm around me.

"Ha, ha." I nudge him away and begin bouncing from one foot to the other with my fists up like a boxer.

"Austria, put 'em down," he says.

"Make me," I reply.

"Seriously, I want you to practice defense moves some more."

"All right, all right."

I stand still. He grabs me from behind. I mock elbow him in the ribs like Camille taught me. I'm afraid that I could do some damage with a real hit. He's already in a cast. Then I mock step on his foot as I turn away and flee.

"Good. Now, Jack, try the handhold move Austria taught you."

Josh grabs Jack's wrist with his good hand. Jack twists his wrist so that his thumb points between where Josh's thumb and forefinger meet. Jack then pulls his wrist out of the hold.

"Nice, Jack," I say.

"Last, I want to see you three make 100 more hits on the most vulnerable parts of the body on the dummies, and then we'll be done. Bring it on and don't hold back. We should practice this every other day for a while so it's ingrained in your thought processes," Emmitt says.

"Really?" I don't continue because the look Josh gives me renders me speechless. We have so much to do as it is. To stop the bad guys and keep each other safe. Do we really have time to be punching dummies? I can see Josh isn't going to back down on this. My voice returns but sounds squeaky like a mouse. "Never mind."

"Austria, you three have to do this in order for us to be able to operate and not worry about you all the time. You also need to train Jack and Camille how to get to the Other World and back. You're not going to be able to make all the trips yourself."

"But, I've already been there two times, Josh. If I take them there to learn, I'll only have one more free trip there."

"This will be your last trip there. I can't risk losing you."

"What? But, Josh?"

"No, this is the last time."

"Fine," I say as I begin my hundred punches. When I'm done, I stalk off to the showers.

My father and I can talk while he's in the Other World and I'm here, but I have yet to learn how to summon him. I would like to know that before I'm unable to return to his world. I like how Josh cares for me enough to want to protect me, but I also can't help feeling a little suffocated when he tells me my next visit is going to be my last. There's got to be a way to figure things out. I have to make sure to spend some quality time with Father and Grandmother this next trip. Maybe we could make the training a weeklong event. It wouldn't be that much time here. I also need to remind Josh that I don't like people trying to control me. I thought I'd made that clear by making the first move.

NAVIGATION

"Okay, so now I need you to rush after it full of anger."

"What? We already exerted ourselves physically with self-defense training," Camille huffs.

"Yeah, I can't get angry at a photo," Jack says.

He's right. While I've travelled on my own to the Other World, I have never planned it out. It just happened while I was enraged with Matt and Ed. They'd also hurt people I cared about, causing my adrenaline to spike. I never had to make it do that on my own. So how can we cause our adrenaline to jump without someone we care about being in danger? Looking at Matt's and Ed's pictures just makes me want to tack them up to the wall and get some dart practice. As I dig through memories trying to formulate something that will get us all to the Other World, pictures flood my head. Football players slapping each other's helmets, psyching up for the game, and female kickboxers smiling through mouth guards while pounding gloves together. Maybe this will work.

"Hey, Jack. So, what're you going to do if they capture Lea and want to use her body as a test to see if a new serum causes mutated Altered Helix organs to not take?" I walk up to Jack and shove him.

"What the?" He looks at me like he's meeting me for the first time. Which I guess is half true as no one here has met this side of me. Shoot, this is the first time I've met this side of me.

"That's it. You're going to protect her with some words. A question." I shove him again. "Come on, Jack. You have more than that. Act like I'm one of them, and I have her tied up behind me. How hard are you going to charge?"

He takes a few deep breaths. He clenches his hands into fists and bounces on the balls of his feet. "If they had her, I'd save her no matter what it took."

Then he charges me. As I brace for the oncoming tackle, he disappears into thin air. It worked. It actually flipping worked.

"He's gone. Did that really happen?" Camille asks.

"Yes, now it's your turn. Emmitt, come here."

Emmitt comes over and stands beside me.

"Camille, what're you going to do if they ever have Emmitt strapped to a gurney?" I grab his wrists with one hand and put my other hand on his throat. I squeeze enough to make his face darken. Camille doesn't say a word as she makes her move toward me. After two running steps, she's gone.

Now I'm up. I can't get myself worked up on my own. Emmitt reads my thoughts and steps toward Josh. He grabs Josh's good arm and puts it behind his back. He puts Josh in a headlock. My heart stops. I don't like how this looks one bit. I run toward them, and nothing happens. I'm about to punch Emmitt in the face when he talks.

"Why didn't you disappear? You too gentle for that sort of thing?"

"I don't know. Probably good, as I wouldn't want to disappear if I were really trying to save Josh. I wonder what the others did differently?"

"Were you thinking about the Other World at all?" Josh asks.

"No, I wasn't. I was only thinking about protecting you. I can change that."

I take a few steps away. Jack and Camille are waiting for me. I close my eyes and breathe in. I imagine the interrogation room Matt and Ed are being held in. Now I imagine Emmitt is Matt when I run toward him. I think of the Other World.

The grassy pad is the same one as the last two visits. I look around and begin feeling the emotions and spinning of this world. I see Camille trying to pet a bird, and Jack has an earthworm in his hand, and he's talking to it.

"Hey, guys. Looks like we made it. Were you two thinking of this world when you charged?"

"Yeah, I was trying to remember what it looked and felt like," Camille says.

"I was just trying to imagine what it was like," Jack says.

"That's key. You have to think about this world and have an adrenaline rush to make it here of your own accord. Oh, and Jack, you don't want to go up those stairs."

He stops where he is and turns around. "Thanks, but why don't I want to climb the stairs?"

"That's how you get to Heaven, and I don't believe you're ready for that."

"Uh, yeah. So what do we do now?"

"Yeah, where's your father?" Camille adds.

"I'm not sure. I was expecting him. Maybe since there was no real danger, he wasn't expecting our visit."

We all begin searching the gorgeous beach, the luscious green grass, and the never-ending staircase into the sky. There isn't another soul to be seen. I begin to feel the spinning sensation again, but, as usual, it doesn't cause nausea. It feels completely natural, as if this has always been where I was meant to be.

Jack looks at me like a lost puppy. "Do you feel that? What is it? Off balance, but not. It's insane."

"We're on a Stranded Coil of a Nebula. So we're spinning at a faster rate than we're accustomed to. Our bodies adapt easily to it because of the Altered Helixes," I explain to him.

"Whoa. That's intense." He reaches down and touches a blade of grass, but doesn't pick it. He must feel their emotions too.

"So what do we do now?" Camille brings us back to the point.

"Well, when I've been here I've been with my father. I concentrated on one of the happiest places and then we appeared there. I'm afraid if we all concentrate on our own favorite places, we'll end up separated. I'm not exactly comfortable with that. Are you guys okay thinking about the house I grew up in?" I ask them, hoping there's no argument.

"What does it look like?" Camille asks. "I've already met your father so I can think about him too."

"Yeah, did you grow up in a mansion or a shack?" Jack asks with a snicker.

I let myself relax a little. Looks like these two won't be arguing with me. Now how to explain my first house? Wait a minute. My mother emailed pictures during the renovation. Can we get an internet connection on a Stranded Coil? I pull out my phone and begin pulling up my email. It states that I've been disconnected from my home Wi-Fi. Kind of figured that would happen. I go to the settings to see what internet's available, if any. One is available called Runner1990. I almost burst into laughter. Thanks, Father. I type in USO-LYMPICGOLD and hit enter. The phone sits with a circle spinning on the screen for quite a while. Then I'm connected. Wow! I stare at the screen in shock for a second before talking.

"Uh guys, I'm connected to the internet. I'm going to pull up some photos of my house so you can envision it," I finally speak out loud.

"What? Really. The internet? So could I email Lea right now?" Jack asks as he leans in toward my phone.

"Let's give it a try," Camille says as both she and Jack pull out their phones and begin to connect.

I share the password with them. As they're attempting to send their emails, a light bulb comes on. Duh! I've been looking for a way to connect with my father while we're worlds apart. I'd never thought to try to use email. Of all the things.

"Here are the pictures, guys. Did your emails go through?"

"Yes. Emmitt just emailed back," Camille says, jumping up and down in excitement.

So my father and I can easily "call" one another. This is wonderful. I begin telling a hide and seek story to Jack and Camille. They looked at the pictures long enough. We're holding hands to be sure we don't lose one another. I close my eyes for a moment and, when I open them, we're in front of the house.

I still can't get over the euphoric feeling of being here. I look at Jack and Camille and smile. They squeeze my hands and smile at me, then release my hands and walk toward the front door. Something's off. Why hasn't anyone sensed us? Why are we still alone? Why are goosebumps prickling up my neck?

A shadow moves behind a corner of the house. I thought I was only going to be haunted by shadows in our world. I grab Camille's and Jack's sleeves to hold them back from approaching the house. I hold my finger up to my mouth in order to hush them. I point to the right corner of the house where I saw the shadow.

"Something isn't right here. I just saw a shadow go behind that corner. Are you guys ready to put some of our self-defense lessons to the test?" I whisper to them.

"What? We haven't been here very long. Are you sure?" Jack asks. I can see the look of disappointment in his eyes. I wish there were another way, but I don't get the feeling that this is going to be a nice visit.

"Did you get any more details than just a shadow?" Camille asks.

"No, I'm sorry, but I really do get the feeling that something is off. My father would be running out the front door to greet us otherwise."

Camille motions for us to quietly follow her. She begins walking to the corner. She stops short and looks back to be sure we're there. She peeks her head around.

The look she gives when she turns back to us is awful. "It's that stupid Adam person and, believe it or not, Matt and Ed are with him. They must have escaped the interrogation your father had set up."

Shoot. This is not good. Do we even risk fighting them? What good would it do?

"Do they have anyone in their possession?" I ask apprehensively.

"No, it's just them."

My muscles relax with her response.

"We should listen and find out what they're up to," Jack says. He's thinking the same thing I am.

"Sounds good. Be ready to fight if they or anyone on their team finds us," I say.

We hide behind the bushes at the front of the house as quietly as we can and begin to listen.

"Told you they were plotting against us," Matt's voice says.

"Don't you think I've made a plan against that? What they are is weak like a bubble floating in the air. All we have to do is poke it and watch it burst," Adam responds.

"They got so much information out of us. Let's face it, they know way too much. What're we going to do?" This comes from Ed.

"Don't worry. Trust me. You must continue to follow my instructions if you don't want your families' fortunes to disappear. I have a backup plan that will blow our competitors right out of the water. While they're jumping over hurdles, I'm going to remove the track on which they plan to land," Adam replies.

With that we hear footsteps approaching. We all sit motionless, attempting to not make a sound. Luckily for us, the footsteps pass. I peer through an opening in the bush to see where they go but, once they're ten steps beyond us, they disappear.

"Are they gone?" Jack asks.

"Yes they are," a voice from beyond the bushes replies.

We all gasp and look to our right. It's the man who spoke so much.

"You all have to get out of here. We're being watched by them, and only the experienced can truly hide."

"I always swing on the tire swing in order to relax and return to our world," I say.

"Perfect. We have three swings out back now just for that."

Jack and Camille look at me.

"We can trust him. Come on, before it's too late."

"But you didn't get to see your father. This is your last trip here." Camille gives me a worried look.

"Hey, no biggie. I can email him now." I give her a friendly shoulder bump and smile, but I really don't feel comforted. She's right. I'm missing some quality time with someone I've missed for years. We should be spending a week of Other World time with him. I'm pissed, but right now we all have to relax in order to return safely. I won't let my desires put them in danger.

We walk to the back yard, take a swing, and begin pumping our legs. It's easy here to get lost in the peaceful emotions of the trees and the clouds. Before we know it, we're back in the gym.

"Well, that was fast. Did you get enough training in?" Emmitt asks as he walks up to Camille and gives her a bear hug.

"Not exactly, but I feel pretty confident of being able to travel if I needed to now," Jack replies.

"What do you mean, not exactly?" Josh asks with his jaw set.

"We weren't able to speak with my father. Matt and Ed had escaped and were talking to Adam," I reply with the most morose look I can muster.

"Yeah, but we learned how to email back and forth from worlds. Did Emmitt show you his email from Camille?" Jack asks.

"Yeah, that was like a minute before you returned," Josh says.

"We need to act fast. Adam said that he has some magnificently horrible plan," Camille interjects.

I take a deep breath. This has all happened so fast and seems to just spiral faster the deeper we get.

SOJOURN

We meet up with everyone at the haunted house, my home away from home. Lea can't sit still as we tell our story to everyone. She also seems to have caught the attachment bug. When an unaltered helix mate fears losing their partner, they seem to be glued to them. She has her hands on Jack nonstop, as if they're fused to him. Sometimes she's holding his hand and sometimes she has a hand on his shoulder while he needs both hands to articulate what he's explaining. Everyone gasps when we tell them we're able to email from the Other World. I normally would be completely exhilarated by all this, but I can't get it out of my head that I didn't get to see my father during my "last" visit.

"Seriously, it's so weird in that world. You feel emotions from everything, even the bees and the birds," Jack exclaims.

Everyone has questions for him about the Other World but Josh. He's getting more rigid as we talk about it. We haven't been effectively communicating since my return. We're on different wavelengths. He has come to terms with the loss of his parents. I haven't come to terms with losing the father I just got back.

"What Adam, Matt, and Ed were talking about scares me. What can their secret plan be? We have to find out, and we have to act fast to complete what we've set out to do. I don't think they're playing easily figured out games. I don't think they ever were. This is serious," Camille exclaims.

Everyone begins chattering. I can't make sense of all the noise. I'm glad to see them all fired up about taking action, but something is stirring within. I know what it is. I have to claim it. My father has the answers, but do I risk communication via email? With the cell-phone companies' disregard of privacy and the government's complete infringement of it, I don't think we can take that risk. I need to communicate with my father face to face. I need to travel back to the Other World.

After the talking dies down, we set plans and dates to complete the surveillance, medical research corruption, and serum administration. It feels nice to know that if all goes as planned, the Altered Helixes of this world and the Other World should be safe. This can only happen if the Altered Helixes in the Other World are able to complete their plans too, but I have a feeling that, if we do our part, they'll be successful.

As the meeting comes to an end, I can't help but wish for just a moment alone, but Josh is having none of that. We all go home, and he's right next to me the entire way. We get ready for bed, but as soon as his breathing slows, and I know he's asleep, I sneak out. I boot up my phone and begin writing an email to an address I never thought would be there. Who knows, it will probably just go to spam and Josh will be happy that I wasn't able to get hold of my father.

"Father,

It's me, Austria. Are you okay? Why were Adam, Matt, and Ed right outside the house? What's going on? Adam mentioned some big plan.

I'm so upset that I didn't get to spend time with you. Josh doesn't want me to ever go back. I hope this email thing works, but Father, I really want to see you again.

I know you want me to have a normal life, but I can visit one more time and still do that. Please respond. I hope this is your email, and you get internet connection too.

Love,

Austria"

I bite my nails as I wait for the response. Ten minutes later, when I'm notified of a message from USOLYMPICGOLD I know it's him and smile as I hide on our porch.

"Austria,

It is not safe now to communicate via email. You can make one last trip here. Wait until Sunday at noon. Grandmother and I will make sure you travel safely, and that we're able to spend some good time to-gether.

I love you too (to the moon and back, and farther)

Father"

We *can* communicate via email. I can set this up on my contacts list and call my father whenever I need him. I've yearned to be able to do that for a very long time.

The days seem to trickle by like sand through an hourglass. I can tell Josh thinks something's up, but I don't care. What he's asking of me is unfair. If our roles were re-versed, I'm sure he'd feel the same way. As

Sunday nears, it's hard to contain my excitement. Sunday morning, Tiff makes breakfast for Luke, Josh, and I. I begin to feel a little guilty, but not enough.

When we finish, I announce that I'm going to the neighborhood nursery to get some evergreen bushes for the front of our condo. I'm tired of seeing all the plants disappear come winter, so it's plausible for me to take this action. Josh automatically volunteers to go with me, but I claim to have a mutual understanding with an employee for a discount; an understanding that would be forfeited if he were there. I don't know how, but a miracle happens and everyone believes me. As I round the corner where I cannot be seen, I instinctively imagine Matt handcuffing Josh, and I also think of seeing my father for the last time. I only have to take one lunge, and I'm there.

The same gosh darn grassy pad. A second later, I'm blinded by light.

"Father?"

"Yes, I'm here."

My eyes adjust, and I see my father. I reach for his hand with mine in the same second. He holds my hand, and I feel as though I'm a child again. All worries of the present day fade into a distant memory.

"Can we play hide and seek in the house again?"

He hesitates. I wonder if this has something to do with Adam, Matt, and Ed being so close to the house last time I was here.

"Sure, honey," he says.

"Are you positive? You hesitated."

"Yes, I'm sure. What else would I want to do during your last visit here?"

He hooks his arm in mine around the elbow as he leads the way. Now I feel like this is as simple as taking a stroll down my own street. I barely even think of the house and then we're there.

"Head on in and hide, if you think you can find a good enough place," my father says as he brushes his fingers across my cheek and smiles at me.

"You're never going to find me," I respond as I take his hand in mine and gaze into his eyes. How did I live so many years without this man there to believe in me unfailingly?

I take a step toward the house. A weight falls on my heart. I con myself into believing it's because this is my last visit, but my subconscious won't let me fully let it go at that.

"Are you sure everything is okay?" I ask.

"Of course, honey, go ahead."

I do, but it feels as though the bones in my legs are made of lead.

I know where I'm going to hide before I even spot the hexagon table. This world has contorted it to fit my current shape and size. Brilliant. I hide inside and wait. And wait. My father has still not come to find me, but then I hear voices.

"Did we really have to meet now?"

"Yes, do you need an event notification and RSVP to discuss saving the Earth?" That's my father's voice.

"Whatever. What do you have that's so urgent it couldn't wait?"

"It's something that could wipe out the entire population of Earth," my father says.

"Are you sure you haven't been hanging around your paranoid group of conspirators too much?"

"I wish. Adam has atomic bomb capabilities. He hasn't only administered serum to the Mutated Altered Helixes to protect their organs, but he's also administered serum that will enable a person to withstand all forms of radiation," my father informs the man.

As the man begins to depart, all I can think is that this is nuts. Atomic weapons, really? Then I remember seeing the articles about a nearby nuclear plant in the newspaper. I can see the picture that went with the article when I close my eyes. Yes, Adam was in the photo. So this is the real deal, as intense as it sounds. What kind of deranged lunatic is this guy? The kind that steals organs and kills people without a moment's hesitation.

"So you're saying that Adam is going to drop an atomic bomb along specific sectors of Earth in order to wipe out all non-Mutated Altered Helixes and ordinary individuals?"

"Yeah, pretty much," my father says grimly.

"Okay, I guess I have to do what I have to do then. Thank you for all of your research. You will be remembered among us even after you're gone. If we survive, we'll be very thankful for your work."

I can't slow my breaths as I hear my father enter the house. He's going to sacrifice himself in order to save us. This just cannot be. I just found how I could communicate with him even when I'm unable to travel here, but if he sacrifices himself, that won't even be a possibility. Does it really have to be this way?

"Ready or not, here I come."

"I'm here." I open the doors of the hexagon table and tumble out. I run up to my father and wrap my arms around him.

"That's not how the game works."

"I don't care. I don't want you to sacrifice yourself."

"Oh, honey, that's just a last-ditch effort. There's only like a .5% chance of it becoming necessary. Don't worry."

"Promise?"

"Promise."

I hug him so tightly I feel as though one of my muscles will snap.

"How about we have one last dinner before you have to go back? We can always discuss more via email. It's more than we've had in so long."

"I know. I just wish you could travel back with me."

"And leave me all alone?" I hadn't noticed my grandmother entering the living room. She has a bag full of groceries.

Father and I help Grandmother cook dinner. We work as a team, as if we've been doing this for years. I wonder if it's because of our DNA similarities. The conversation is fairly pleasant, but I'm still bothered by the previous revelation.

"Grandmother? What do you think of this Adam guy? What do you think of his plan?"

"I think we have it under control is what I think, sugar bear."

"Are you sure? I mean, he's messing with nuclear stuff."

"Sugar bear, it's fine. We can handle more than you give us credit for."

I slump my shoulders and begin scrubbing some of the pots in the sink. It seems as though I'm not going to get through to either one of them. I should really just enjoy this visit. I take a deep breath and grab the dishes to set the table. My father pats me on the back as I pass. Dinner smells good. I feel starved, even though I know it's only my psyche. I keep looking at them both, trying to memorize their features.

"Do you remember when your father tried cooking the Thanksgiving turkey? I think you were about eight."

"I'm not sure. I do remember there being a lot of smoke in the kitchen once. Was that because of his cooking?"

"Hey, that was my first time cooking a turkey. Would you cut me a break?" My father begs.

"He burnt that turkey to a crisp."

"What did we end up doing?"

"Luckily, Walmart was open, and we were able to swing by and purchase a couple of rotisserie chickens."

"We still had the loveliest time." Now it's my grandmother's turn to pat my father on the back.

"That was the year you taught me hop-scotch." I remember my father hopping on the squares like a little girl would. I thought it was so silly but was thrilled that I would be able to join the girls at school.

"That's right, honey. You picked it up pretty fast. I was so proud of you. I am proud of you. You have become a beautiful, intelligent, and caring young woman." My father has tears in his eyes.

"Thank you, Father. I've always loved you, and I always will." Now I have tears in my eyes.

"There, there, you two. I'm proud of both of you and love you to pieces." My grandmother brings us in for a group hug. I smile at her, and she smiles at me. Then I peek at my father, and he smiles at me too.

"Well, well, looks like it's about time for you to get back on the swing." My grandmother smooths her apron and clears her throat. She gives my father a look.

He just grabs me in a bear hug. Then we all head to the swing. I have to breathe slowly to keep from bursting into tears. I sit on the tire and let them get me going. Then I pump my legs and force myself to relax by thinking of the smiles they gave me in the group hug.

FINALE

I awake in bed with Josh. Oh, he's going to be furious. I don't want to wake him, but I'd like to brush my teeth and put on my pajamas. I get out of bed softly and tiptoe to the lamp on the other side of the room. I get my pajamas out of the dresser quietly and put them on. As I look at Josh, I see tear streaks running down his cheeks. He cried himself to sleep. Shoot, I didn't mean to worry him that much. I turn off the light and head to the bathroom. I brush my teeth as quickly as I can and tiptoe back to bed. I gently get back under the covers without waking Josh. I put my arm around him and hold him close. He doesn't say a word but grabs my hand and squeezes. He rubs circles on the back of my hand with his thumb. After a couple minutes, he stops, and his breathing slows. He's asleep. Now, will I be able to fall as easily as he did?

That's when I notice the light on my phone blinking. I must have an email. I left it by the lamp and have to get up to retrieve it. I grab my phone and unlock it. When I pull up my email, I find a message from my father, already. Time does travel at different rates between his world and mine. I wonder if the email time stamp will reflect that. The subject line is "I love you." I click on the message. The time is the same as here. Interesting. This is what the message says:

"Austria,

It was so good to see you, honey. I have enjoyed the past few visits you've had here. I will always be rooting you on. I'm so happy you get to live the life I wasn't able to. We can win this fight against our enemies. Promise you'll enjoy your life. I will be honest. If this feels like a goodbye it's because it is. Adam is taking initiative on

*the nuclear plan. If I strike now, I can stop
him. Please watch over Mother for me and
tell her I love her.*

Love,

Father"

I instantly hit the reply button and begin
typing. "You can tell her yourself because
I will not let you do this." Before I hit another key, I stop. If I send him that message,
he'll know what I'm going to do. I can't
risk it. I can't believe he's actually going to
do this to me again. He doesn't want to, but
he's leaving me. Recurring feelings of
abandonment wash over me. Then I remember my dream conversation with
Grandmother: *You have to let him go, child.
All he wants is for you to have a life. You'll
understand one day when you have children of your own.* Did he and Grandmother
know all along? I can't let him do this. I
need him in my life. There has to be another
way. Can I find Adam and stop him myself? Will that save my father? It would

take too much time. I've already lost quite a bit since the time passes differently there than here. I have to go to the Other World. That's the only way I can stop him. But this will now be my fifth and last trip. Did he let me make the previous visit on purpose, believing I would be incapable of interfering with this suicide plan of his?

I look at Josh and drop to my knees. I didn't mind leaving for a visit with Father, but this time I'll be leaving him for good. Pain sears through my chest. What will this do to him? The tears that had welled up in my eyes on the swing burst past my eyelids now. Why does it have to be like this? The only way to save my father is to travel to the Other World and stop him. By doing that, I will leave Josh, my mother, and my whole haunted house family behind. Or I can stay here with Josh, my first true love, and lose my father, who I just got back, forever. It's not fair. I get the feeling that, as you grow up, you find out that more and more is unfair. I stand as I weigh the options in my head. Allow my father to sacrifice himself or make Josh heartbroken? You can heal from heartbreak. You can't heal from suicide. I know what I must do.

I write Josh a note. Not really my ideal way of saying goodbye, but if I wake him, he'll try to stop me.

"Josh,

I'm so sorry for upsetting you and visiting my father. I hope you can forgive me for that and for what I'm about to do. It was a miracle finding you. I love you so much. Please live a happy life. This is the only way to honor our love. I have to go back to the Other World to save my father. Tell everyone I'm an email away and will help continue the fight against our enemies. You can email me too, but I understand if you don't want to. You're the best man on Earth I know.

Love,
Austria"

Ugh, that's awful. I can't come up with better right now, and I'm short on time. Maybe I can send an email after I save my father. Josh is going to hate this no matter what I say. I hope he understands. I hope he sees that, if things were reversed, I would understand. My hands shake as I fold the note and put it on my pillow. I want to gather him in my arms and hold him one last time, but I can't find the strength. I feel like I could faint. I have to take a deep breath. I turn around and think about Adam. Why do evil, power-hungry people like him have to exist? I think of the Other World. I angrily think of what I would do to Adam if he were here now. Then I run two steps as if Adam were in front of me, and I could tackle him. This is it. "Goodbye!" I begin to feel the spinning and unexplainable emotions of the Other World I'm drifting to. Funny how it seems like I had just struggled to hang onto life recently and now here I am floating away from it voluntarily.

ACKNOWLEDGMENTS

The transformation this novella has been through would not have been possible without many people. There's no way I can name them all but I'd like to give it a try. They know how hard I've worked and how many years I've dedicated to books. First, I would like to thank the readers. You breathe life into books and for that I will be ever thankful. Next, I would like to thank the professionals that helped me trudge through this thing called publishing: everyone at Hypothesis Productions, Sheri Williams, Nancy Schumacher, Caroline Andrus, Kelsey Skea, Jennifer Newens, Callie Metler-Smith, Georgia McBride, Leanne Tavares, Erica Christensen, and Karen Lynch. Next, I would like to thank my friends who saw me through dark times and helped me celebrate the good times too: Shana Bartlett, James Young, Miranda Nichols, Amy Garton, Stacked Book Club, Sarah Smith, and Cathy Wissing. Finally, I would like to thank my family for putting up with me: Nate, Ethan, Jenna, Vic Hurlbert, Debra Scarborough, Cassandra Hurlbert, Victor Hurlbert, Vondell Neill, and Peggy Hurlbert. If I inadvertently left someone off the list please let me know so I can add them to the next book.

ABOUT THE AUTHOR

Stephanie Hansen's short story, Break Time, and poetry has been featured in Mind's Eye literary magazine. The Kansas Writers Association published her short story, Existing Forces, appointing her as a noted author. She has held a deep passion for writing since early childhood, but a brush with death caused her to allow it to grow. She's part of an SCBWI critique group in Lawrence, KS and two local book clubs. She attends many writers' conferences including the New York Pitch, Penned Con, New Letters, All Write Now, Show Me Writers Master Class, BEA, and Nebraska Writers Guild conference as well as Book Fairs and Comic-Cons. She's a member of the deaf and hard of hearing community. https://www.authorstepha-niehansen.com/

www.ingramcontent.com/pod-product-compliance
Lightning Source LLC
Chambersburg PA
CBHW030741110726
47900CB00008B/2398